A MEXICAN-AMERICAN STANDOFF

Fargo's hand fell on Guillermo's shoulder. "Let the young lady go."

Guillermo struck Fargo's hand aside. "How dare you touch me, gringo?" He reached for the gun on his hip.

The fingers of Fargo's left hand clamped hard around Guillermo's wrist. The young man gasped in pain as the fingers of his gun hand involuntarily splayed out, unable to grasp the butt of his revolver.

Behind Fargo, the metallic ratcheting of a gun being cocked punctuated a harsh command. "Unhand my son, señor, or I will be forced to shoot you."

Fargo glanced back and saw Victorio Soto pointing a heavy old cap-and-ball pistol at him. From the corner of his eye, Fargo saw Colonel Drummond aim his Colt at Soto and say, "Drop that gun, mister, right now."

Everyone else in the dining room sat in tense silence, waiting to see what was going to happen. Fargo knew that the room was a powder keg—and all it needed was the tiniest spark to make it blow all to hell. . . .

THE TRAILSMAN

#337

SILVER SHOWDOWN

by

Jon Sharpe

A SIGNET BOOK

SIGNET
Published by New American Library, a division of
Penguin Group (USA) Inc., 375 Hudson Street,
New York, New York 10014, USA
Penguin Group (Canada), 90 Eglinton Avenue East, Suite 700, Toronto,
Ontario M4P 2Y3, Canada (a division of Pearson Penguin Canada Inc.)
Penguin Books Ltd., 80 Strand, London WC2R 0RL, England
Penguin Ireland, 25 St. Stephen's Green, Dublin 2,
Ireland (a division of Penguin Books Ltd.)
Penguin Group (Australia), 250 Camberwell Road, Camberwell, Victoria 3124,
Australia (a division of Pearson Australia Group Pty. Ltd.)
Penguin Books India Pvt. Ltd., 11 Community Centre, Panchsheel Park,
New Delhi - 110 017, India
Penguin Group (NZ), 67 Apollo Drive, Rosedale, North Shore 0632,
New Zealand (a division of Pearson New Zealand Ltd.)
Penguin Books (South Africa) (Pty.) Ltd., 24 Sturdee Avenue,
Rosebank, Johannesburg 2196, South Africa

Penguin Books Ltd., Registered Offices:
80 Strand, London WC2R 0RL, England

First published by Signet, an imprint of New American Library,
a division of Penguin Group (USA) Inc.

First Printing, November 2009
10 9 8 7 6 5 4 3 2 1

The first chapter of this book previously appeared in *Utah Outlaws*, the three hundred
thirty-sixth volume in this series.

Copyright © Penguin Group (USA) Inc., 2009

 REGISTERED TRADEMARK—MARCA REGISTRADA

Printed in the United States of America

Wi⟨...⟩ublication may
be ⟨...⟩ any form, or
by ⟨...⟩), without the
pri⟨...⟩of this book.

PUB⟨...⟩
Thi⟨...⟩e the product
of t⟨...⟩o actual per-
son⟨...⟩oincidental.

ity ⟨...⟩responsibil-

If yo⟨...⟩should be aware that this book is stolen
property. It was reported as "unsold and destroyed" to the publisher and neither the
author nor the publisher has received any payment for this "stripped book."

The scanning, uploading, and distribution of this book via the Internet or via any other
means without the permission of the publisher is illegal and punishable by law. Please
purchase only authorized electronic editions, and do not participate in or encourage electronic piracy of copyrighted materials. Your support of the author's rights is appreciated.

The Trailsman

Beginnings . . . they bend the tree and they mark the man. Skye Fargo was born when he was eighteen. Terror was his midwife, vengeance his first cry. Killing spawned Skye Fargo, ruthless, cold-blooded murder. Out of the acrid smoke of gunpowder still hanging in the air, he rose, cried out a promise never forgotten.

The Trailsman they began to call him all across the West: searcher, scout, hunter, the man who could see where others only looked, his skills for hire but not his soul, the man who lived each day to the fullest, yet trailed each tomorrow. Skye Fargo, the Trailsman, the seeker who could take the wildness of a land and the wanting of a woman and make them his own.

*Nevada Territory, 1861—where men vie for silver,
and the Trailsman deals in lead.*

1

The keen senses of the big man in buckskins didn't miss much. But so much hell was breaking loose on the other side of the ridge, Skye Fargo figured a fella would have to be both deaf and blind to have missed it.

His lake blue eyes narrowed as he studied the clouds of dust rising into the crystal clear Nevada sky. Pounding hoofbeats, thundering guns, and strident yells filled the air. Fargo, a powerfully built man in buckskins and a broad-brimmed brown hat, hauled his horse's head around and sent the magnificent black-and-white Ovaro stallion galloping to the top of the ridge. He pulled his Henry rifle from its saddle sheath as horse and rider neared the crest.

Fargo topped the rise. The far side of the ridge sloped down to a broad flat. This southern section of Nevada Territory was rocky, semiarid country, a land of tans and browns and grays with only occasional splashes of green where stubborn vegetation had taken hold.

Three wagons, each drawn by a team of six mules, had been crossing that flat when a group of hombres firing six-guns had jumped them. Fargo read that story as plainly as if it had been printed in a book. The wagons passed by below him, heading from his left to his right.

The dust billowing up from the wagon wheels and the hooves of mules and horses made it difficult for him to be sure, but he thought at least a dozen men were giving chase to the wagons. The vehicles had canvas covers stretched from sideboard to sideboard, covering some sort of cargo. These were freight wagons, not the prairie schooners used by immigrants in their journeys westward across the American frontier.

Even though the terrain looked flat from a distance, it really wasn't. Fargo knew that gullies cut across it, and little ridges and hummocks and depressions broke it up. Because of that, the wagons jolted heavily and swayed from side to side as they careened along. The drivers had their hands full as they lashed those mules on in a desperate effort to escape from the men who had attacked them.

The driver was the only man on each of the first two wagons. A pair of men rode the third vehicle. One man handled the reins while the other knelt atop whatever the freight was. He had a rifle he was using to fire at the pursuers, but it was a single-shot weapon. The man had to reload after every round.

And then he couldn't even do that, because he dropped the rifle, clutched his chest with both hands, and toppled off the swaying wagon. He landed in a heap on the ground, and a second later the riders trampled right over him, never slowing down or veering their mounts as the steel-shod hooves slashed the unfortunate man to ribbons.

The sight of that wanton savagery removed any doubt from Fargo's mind about who was in the right here. Those horsebackers were no-good varmints and needed to be dealt with accordingly.

They were all past him now. He wheeled the Ovaro and sent the stallion racing along the top of the ridge, riding a parallel course. Just like the riders were gaining ground on the slower wagons, so too was the Ovaro catching up to the would-be robbers. Fargo was convinced the men were trying to steal whatever was in the wagons.

He could have blazed away at them from behind, but the idea of shooting anybody in the back didn't sit well with him. He drew even with the attackers and began angling down the ridge toward them.

Some of them saw him coming and must have figured that he was a threat, because gun smoke began to spurt from their weapons toward him. At that sight, a fighting grin creased Fargo's tanned, bearded face.

They had opened the ball. Now he would call the tune.

Guiding the stallion with his knees, he brought the Henry to his shoulder and cranked off three shots as fast as he could work the repeater's lever. Only one of the men threw up his arms and pitched out of the saddle, but Fargo's shots served their purpose. He had distracted the thieves and served notice that he was a danger to them.

The group split up, four men peeling off to come charging toward him with guns blazing. It was always a good thing, Fargo thought, when you could get your enemies to divide their forces.

Now he was only outnumbered four to one.

He spotted a cluster of boulders and angled the stallion toward the rocks, intending to fort up there and try to hold off the gunmen. Before he could reach the boulders, though, a dull boom sounded, and one of the men went flying out of the saddle as if he had just run headlong into a stone wall.

That made the other three rein in sharply, as they seemed to be trying to figure out what was going on and where that booming shot had come from. Fargo took advantage of the opportunity to whip the Henry to his shoulder and send several more rounds whistling their way. One of the men grabbed his shoulder and slew sideways in the saddle, but he managed to stay mounted as all three of them gave up the fight. They whirled their horses around and galloped after the others.

The boom sounded again. Fargo recognized it as the report of a Sharps Big Fifty. He knew it quite well, because he had carried one of the high-powered, large-caliber rifles for years before switching to the newer Henry repeater. He looked to his right along the ridge and saw that another rider had topped it. The man's horse stood still under him as he finished reloading, raised the Sharps to his shoulder, and fired again.

Two more of the outlaws were down. Whoever was using that buffalo gun was a damned good shot with it, thought Fargo. He kept using the Henry to pepper the men who had been pursuing the wagons, spacing his shots to alternate with the Sharps. Several more of the outlaws clutched broken shoulders or punctured arms.

They gave up the fight, yanked their horses around, and pounded off toward the north. The wagons kept moving east across the flat, but they slowed now that the immediate threat seemed to be over.

Soon Fargo couldn't see anything of the outlaws except a dwindling cloud of dust. Four of the men were down, lying motionless on the ground. Fargo rode toward them. He had a hunch they were all dead, but he wanted to be sure.

As he approached the men, he saw the rider with the Sharps coming toward him, and a shock of recognition went through him as he realized that he knew the man. "Jim McLeod!" Fargo exclaimed. "Is that really you?"

The man reined in and grinned at him through a bushy, gray-shot beard. "Why shouldn't it be me?" he demanded in a voice that boomed almost as loudly as the Sharps he carried. "Did you think I was dead or somethin', Skye?"

"You're old enough. I wouldn't have been surprised." Fargo moved his horse closer to McLeod's and reached out to clasp the man's hand in a firm grip. "It's mighty good to see you again, you old snapping turtle. And I'm obliged for the helping hand."

McLeod wore buckskins that were dark with age, sweat,

and grease. His massive shoulders and arms strained the shirt. He took off his gray floppy-brimmed felt hat, revealing a mostly bald head, and fanned himself with it, saying, "It's a lot hotter down here than it is in the high country."

Fargo smiled. It was just like old Jim to ignore a word of thanks. He never had taken gratitude well, or a compliment, either, for that matter. So Fargo gave him one by saying, "That was some powerful-good shooting you just did."

McLeod grunted. "You, too," he said. He gestured with a hamlike hand toward the nearest of the dead men. "You know those hombres?"

Fargo moved the Ovaro closer and looked down at the corpse, studying the lean, wolflike, beard-stubbled face. After a moment he shook his head.

"Can't say as I've ever seen him before, but I know the type."

"Yeah," McLeod agreed. "Damned desperado. Him and those other hardcases were tryin' to hold up those wagons."

"That's what I think, too," Fargo agreed with a nod. He looked toward the east, where the wagons had come to a stop, turned around, and were now rolling back toward him and McLeod at a much more deliberate pace. "I guess we can ask those fellas what it's all about."

While they waited, Fargo checked the bodies of the other robbers and confirmed that they were dead, too. Then he thought about the last time he had seen Jim McLeod.

Jim was one of the old-time mountain men, a fur trapper who had first come west forty years earlier when the frontier belonged almost completely to the Indians. Except for occasional trips back to Saint Louis to sell his pelts, he had been out here ever since. Whenever the fur trade had gone through lean times, McLeod had made a living guiding wagon trains or working for the army as a scout, jobs that Fargo had also taken on from time to time.

Fargo had run into him several times over the years. They had always gotten along well. Although McLeod was considerably older, they were kindred spirits who felt most at home far from civilization.

The last time they had met was a couple of years earlier in Santa Fe. McLeod had made an enemy of some Mexican bravo whose family had been around the settlement since Spain controlled what was now New Mexico Territory. Fargo didn't know what the fight was over—probably a woman, considering that Jim had an eye for the ladies—but he had pitched in to help when McLeod found himself in a back-alley brawl with half a dozen men intent on beating him within an inch of his life.

It had been a good fight. McLeod couldn't throw a punch without yelling at the top of his lungs, so it had been a noisy one, too. In the end, Fargo and McLeod had stood battered and bloody but unbowed with their enemies heaped senseless around them. Fargo had to grin just thinking about it now.

The wagons came to a stop a few yards away. Fargo still couldn't see what was under the canvas covers. The driver of the lead wagon, who had a gray spade beard, wrapped the reins around the brake lever and hopped lithely to the ground, despite being middle-aged. He walked over to Fargo and McLeod and reached up to shake hands with them.

"My thanks, gentlemen," he said in a brusque tone. "Without your intervention, those brigands likely would have killed us all. I'm Colonel Henry Drummond, at your service."

"Are you on active duty, Colonel?" Fargo asked. He hadn't heard of Drummond before.

"No, sir. I'm retired. Actually, I resigned my commission to pursue other endeavors." Drummond swept a hand toward the wagons.

"Starting a freight company?"

"Oh, it's more than that," Drummond assured them. "Mr. . . . ?"

"Fargo. Skye Fargo."

"And I'm Jim McLeod," the old mountain man put in. He jerked a thumb at Fargo. "You might know Skye here better as the Trailsman. Folks stuck that moniker on him a while back when they realized there ain't nobody out here on the frontier better at followin' an old trail or findin' a new one."

Drummond's iron gray eyebrows rose. "Indeed, I have heard of you, Mr. Fargo," he said. "I'm fortunate that you two men came along at just the right moment to save me and my wagons from those outlaws."

"You're doubly lucky," Fargo said, "because Jim and I weren't traveling together. We just happened to come along at the same time."

"That's only true if you believe in coincidence. I don't." A solemn expression came over Drummond's face as he went on. "I just wish providence had sent you to us in time to save my guards. I had one man on every wagon, in addition to the driver. I think they were all killed."

"We'll go see about that," Fargo said. "Come on, Jim."

They turned their horses and rode back along the route the wagons had followed. Within a few hundred yards, they had found all three bodies. Drummond's grim prediction was right: the guards were all dead.

When they rode back to the wagons and reported the news to Drummond, the colonel sent his other two men back with one of the wagons to pick up the bodies. "We'll give them decent burials when we get back to the settle-

7

ment," Drummond said. "It's the least we can do for the poor men."

"What settlement are you talking about?" Fargo asked. "I didn't know there was one near here."

"It hasn't been there long," Drummond explained, "only since silver was discovered in the hills a few months ago. A few Mormons lived there before that, near some springs called Las Vegas. That's what people have started calling the town, too."

Fargo nodded. He recalled hearing something about a settlement known as Las Vegas down here in this corner of Nevada Territory, but he hadn't been there yet.

He remembered those springs from earlier trips through this part of the country, though. They were one of the few dependable sources of water in the mostly arid landscape.

"What's this about silver in the hills?"

McLeod replied to Fargo's question before Drummond could. "You ain't heard about the strike, Skye? Folks claim there's as much silver in those hills over west of here as there was gold in California back in 'forty-nine. That's why I was headin' in that direction. I intend to find out for myself."

Fargo frowned in surprise. "You're turning into a prospector, Jim? I remember you telling me that the fellas who went to California during the gold rush were the biggest damn fools under the sun. You said a precious few of them would get rich, and all the rest would break their backs for nothing."

"And that's pretty much the way it worked out, ain't it?"

"Pretty much," Fargo agreed with a shrug.

McLeod pointed toward the hills rising several miles away, at the western end of the flat. "Well, this is different. I can feel it in my bones. Which are a heap older than they were back in 'forty-nine, by the way. I'm gettin' too old to go scroungin' around for jobs. I want to make my fortune and be done with it." He grinned at Drummond. "What do you think, Colonel? Is this the place to do it?"

"That remains to be seen," Drummond said, "but so far all the signs point to this being a significant strike. Perhaps not on the same level as the Comstock Lode, up in the northern part of the territory . . . but the silver barons have already moved in up there. Things are still wide-open down here, and the ore I've been taking out of my mine is good enough to attract the attention of thieves and highwaymen like those you encountered earlier."

"That's silver ore you've got in the back of those wagons," Fargo guessed.

Drummond nodded. "That's correct."

"If you don't mind my asking, what do you do with it once you've gotten it to Las Vegas?"

"Not at all. Since it's intended for United States coins, an army detail picks it up. From there it continues under military escort to the mint in San Francisco. The only real problem is getting it from the mine to Las Vegas."

"You've had problems with outlaws before?"

Drummond nodded curtly. "You could say that. Starting out, I sent a single wagon at a time to the settlement. I lost three of them, and the drivers and guards were all murdered. So I decided to buy more wagons and take a larger group of them in, figuring that would be safer. The first three made it safely. But I suppose the gang that's been causing all the trouble recruited more members, because they attacked this wagon train."

Fargo thought that "wagon train" was a pretty grand name for a group of only three wagons, but he supposed Drummond could call it whatever he wanted to.

"Why don't Jim and I ride on into town with you, just

9

in case those varmints decide to come back?" Fargo suggested.

"Speak for yourself, Skye," McLeod rumbled. "I'm on my way to the mountains to prospect for silver my ownself, remember?"

"I'll make it worth your while to delay your efforts for a few days, Mr. McLeod," the colonel said. "I'll certainly feel better about making it to Las Vegas with you two along."

"Well . . ." McLeod scratched his bristly beard. "I reckon I could do that. A little extra money would help me get myself a better stake 'fore I start out."

"It's agreed, then."

The wagon Drummond had sent to fetch the bodies of the dead guards returned. The two men had laid out the corpses on top of the canvas-covered ore in the back.

Within a few minutes, all three vehicles were rolling east again. Fargo and McLeod rode alongside the first one, with Colonel Drummond handling the reins.

Las Vegas was only about five miles away, the colonel explained, so they would be there well before dark. That prediction proved to be true. The trees and grass growing around the springs came into view. That vegetation had given the place its name, which meant "the meadows," and it was a welcome oasis in this near-wasteland.

The settlement consisted of about two dozen buildings made of stone, adobe, and timber. The largest and, judging by appearances, newest building had a sign across its front with the name Silver Queen Saloon emblazoned on it.

No, this definitely wasn't a Mormon settlement anymore, Fargo thought as he saw that.

Then the sight of someone running out of the hotel across the street from the saloon caught his attention. The figure belonged to a woman—a beautiful young woman with long, thick hair as black as a raven's wing. She ran up to the horses, caught hold of Jim McLeod's leg as he reined in, and cried joyously, "Papa!"

Fargo grinned over at the old mountain man and said, "Looks like there's something you forgot to mention, Jim."

2

"Reckon I had a good reason not to mention it, the kind o' reputation you got with the gals, Skye," McLeod muttered. He reached down and patted the young woman's shoulder. "This here is my daughter Rosa. Rosa, meet Skye Fargo."

Rosa smiled up at Fargo, her dark eyes sparkling in her olive-skinned face. She was in her early twenties, he judged, and very attractive. Although the simple gray wool dress she wore was modestly high-necked and long-sleeved, it did little to conceal the ample curves of her body.

Fargo tugged on the brim of his Stetson and said, "Pleased to meet you, Miss McLeod."

"I've heard my father speak of you," she said. "You are the one who is known as the Trailsman?"

Fargo nodded. "That's right." He glanced over at Drummond, who had brought the first wagon to a halt. The other two stopped behind him. Fargo figured the silver ore was safe enough now that the wagons had reached Las Vegas. "We'll see you later, Colonel."

"Come by my office," Drummond said, pointing to a frame building down the street with a sign on it that read DRUMMOND MINING COMPANY. "I said I'd make it worth your while for assisting me, gentlemen, and I intend to honor that pledge."

Fargo didn't think that he and McLeod had done all that much, but if Drummond wanted to pay them a little for their help, he wasn't going to argue with the man. McLeod had said that he could use a bigger stake before he set out on his prospecting trip, and Fargo's own poke was a mite skimpy these days. He had planned to replenish it with a few hands of poker in the next settlement he came to.

That had turned out to be Las Vegas, and from the looks of the Silver Queen, he would be able to find a game there. It wouldn't hurt if he had a bigger stake of his own, though, when he sat down at the table.

"How long have you been here?" McLeod asked his daughter. "Was that money I sent you enough to get you a room at the hotel?"

"I'm saving the money," Rosa said with a smile. "I got a job at the hotel as a maid, instead. That way my room is free."

"Dadgum it, gal!" McLeod rumbled. "When I wrote to you and asked you to meet up with me here, I didn't expect you to have to do that."

"I didn't have to. It was my choice. I spent what I needed to in order to get here, but I thought you'd be able to use any money that was left over."

"That's mighty thoughtful of you. I want to make life better for you, though. That's why I sent for you, instead o' lettin' you stay in Santa Fe after your ma died."

Rosa nodded. "I know. But we will work together, Papa. There's no reason I can't help you look for silver."

McLeod's bushy eyebrows lifted in surprise. "You're plannin' to come prospectin' with me? Damn it—I mean, dadgum it—those hills ain't any sort o' place for a gal!"

From the determined look on Rosa's face, Fargo figured the old mountain man was in for an argument. Not wanting to risk getting caught in the middle of it, he nodded toward the Silver Queen and said, "I think I'll wet my whistle, Jim. See you later."

"Hold on a minute," McLeod said. "I'll come with you." He turned back to Rosa. "You go back to the hotel. I'll talk to you after a while, and we'll hash all this out."

Her chin had a defiant tilt as she said, "You mean you'll order me to go along with whatever you want?"

"I *am* your father."

"No one would know that, the way you've barely acknowledged my existence all these years."

McLeod winced. Fargo felt a pang of sympathy for him. He didn't have any young'uns of his own, but he remembered that verse from Shakespeare about the tongue of a thankless child being sharper than a serpent's tooth.

But maybe Rosa was justified in feeling the way she did, he reminded himself. He didn't know the story of her relationship with McLeod, and he didn't want to. It was none of his business. He tugged the Ovaro's head around and rode over to the hitch rail in front of the saloon.

McLeod followed him. They tied up their horses and went inside. The thick stone and timber walls of the Silver Queen meant that it was cool in the saloon, a welcome relief from the heat outside. Fargo and McLeod headed for the long bar that ran down the right side of the big main room.

They ordered beers from a slender, sallow-faced bartender. McLeod took a long swallow from his, used the back of his hand to wipe suds from his mustache, and then sighed.

"I reckon you're gonna want to hear about Rosa, ain't you, Skye?" he asked.

"I'm a mite curious," Fargo admitted. "We haven't spent all that much time together, but as I recall, you never said anything about having a daughter."

McLeod motioned with his beer mug toward an empty table. "Let's sit down, and I'll tell you about it."

When they had sat down at the table and started sipping on their beers, the old mountain man went on. "I met Rosa's mama a long time ago in Santa Fe. Back then the Mexicans were still runnin' things there, but a lot of American trappers brought their pelts there to trade. I did, too, sometimes, and it was on one o' them trips that I met Madelina Montez."

"Rosa's mother," Fargo guessed.

McLeod nodded. "She was supposed to marry an hombre named Victorio Soto, but me and her fell in love and run off to get hitched. By the time Soto found out about it, it was too late for him to do anything about it. I don't reckon he ever forgave either of us, though." McLeod paused for another sip of beer, then added, "He was an evil son of a bitch, too. I always worried that he'd try to get back at Madelina while I was off in the mountains trappin', but he never did. He married some other poor gal and made life miserable for her instead."

Fargo leaned forward in his chair and frowned. "Wait a minute," he said. "Did this old grudge have anything to do with that ruckus a couple of years ago?"

"It had ever'thing to do with it," McLeod confirmed. "The fella who started it was Guillermo Soto, old Victorio's son. I reckon he grew up bein' taught to hate me. When he started tryin' to court Rosa a couple o' years ago, I knew he planned to hurt her so's he could get back at me for what I done to his pa."

"Maybe he was actually interested in her," Fargo suggested. "Rosa's a beautiful young woman."

"Yeah, but Guillermo's too steeped in hate to have anything else inside him. I laid down the law, told him to steer clear o' Rosa, and you saw what happened. Him and some o' his pards jumped me in an alley. They might've killed me if you hadn't taken cards in the game, Skye."

Fargo thought about it and decided that McLeod was right. There had been a particular savagery in the attack that elevated it to more than just a simple brawl in a cantina.

"Anyway," McLeod went on, "when Madelina passed away a while back, I knew I couldn't leave Rosa there in Santa Fe to fend for herself, not with Guillermo sniffin' around her the way he was bound to be. I trusted Madelina to keep Rosa safe, but with her gone . . ." The mountain man's massive shoulders rose and fell. "Seemed like it'd be best to have her with me, even though the life I lead ain't really one that's fittin' for a gal."

"That's probably wise," Fargo said. "It might be a good idea to convince her to stay here in the settlement, though, instead of roaming around the hills with you."

McLeod nodded solemnly. "That's what I was thinkin'. But you don't know that gal, Skye. Convincin' her of somethin' when she don't want to be convinced is one hell of a job."

Having seen the fire in Rosa McLeod's eyes, Fargo could easily imagine that was true.

He leaned back in his chair and chuckled. "Here all these years I thought you were quite a charmer with the ladies, and all the time you were an old married man."

"Hell, just 'cause a fella's married don't mean he can't have a twinkle in his eye when he's talkin' to the gals. I never busted my vows to Madelina, though. That twinkle was as far as it ever went."

Fargo believed him. He heard the sincerity in McLeod's voice and saw it in the mountain man's gaze.

McLeod lifted his mug and drained the rest of the beer, then set the empty on the table with a thump. He belched and said, "Reckon I'd better get on over to the hotel and see if I can talk Rosa into bein' reasonable. Wish me luck, Skye."

"Good luck," Fargo said. "I have a hunch you'll need it."

McLeod just rolled his eyes and nodded.

Fargo finished off his beer and left the saloon, too. As he paused outside, his eye happened to fall on Colonel Drummond's office down the street. The colonel had told him and McLeod to stop by there later. Fargo supposed he might as well pay Drummond a visit now and get it over with.

When Fargo entered the building, he found that it contained two desks, one in front of a gated railing and the other behind it. He was a little surprised to see a woman sitting at the desk in front of the railing.

In a frontier settlement the size of Las Vegas, it wasn't uncommon to find very few women, maybe none at all. And often the only females in a town would be the soiled doves who worked at the local saloon. In Las Vegas, Rosa McLeod didn't fall into that category, and neither did this woman, who was using a pen and ink to write figures in an open ledger book.

She glanced up at him through a pair of spectacles and asked, "Yes? Can I help you, sir?"

"Colonel Drummond asked me to stop by. My name is Skye Fargo."

Recognition dawned in her eyes. "You're one of the men who helped Henry when those bandits attacked the wagons! He told me all about it. If not for you and your friend, Henry and his drivers would have been killed, too, just like those poor guards."

"Would you happen to be Mrs. Drummond, ma'am?" Fargo asked. The woman was considerably younger than the colonel, probably around thirty years old, but a lot of men had younger wives.

The question prompted a laugh. "No, but I'm Miss Drummond. Henry is my brother. My name is Lily."

Fargo touched a finger to the brim of his hat. "I'm pleased to meet you," he said. "Is the colonel here?"

"No, he's gone down the street to talk to the undertaker." A solemn look came over Lily Drummond's face. "There are arrangements to make, you know."

"Of course," Fargo said. "Well, if you'll tell him that I stopped by . . ."

Lily came to her feet and said, "You can wait for him here if you'd like. You won't bother me. I'm just entering some figures in the records." She smiled. "Henry is a firm believer in keeping good records. He was a staff officer, you know. He served in the Mexican War, and then he was posted out here for several years. That's why he knows so much about the area."

That was more than Fargo really needed to know about Drummond's military career. He didn't want to be rude to Lily, though. For one thing, she was a nice-looking woman, with honey-colored hair pulled back in a tight bun behind her head and a slender body in a demure dark blue dress, and Fargo enjoyed talking with her.

The door opened behind him, and when Fargo glanced around, he saw Drummond coming into the office. The colonel nodded to him and said, "Good to see you again, Mr. Fargo. I was hoping you'd stop by. Come into my office so we can talk."

He opened the gate in the railing and held out a hand to usher Fargo through it. Fargo suppressed a smile. Drummond sounded completely serious, despite the fact that nothing separated the two desks except the waist-high railing.

Drummond went behind the second desk while Fargo sat down in a ladder-back chair in front of it. The colonel took off the flat-brimmed hat he wore and set it on the desk. "I've been down at the undertaker's," he said. "Arrangements to make, you know."

Fargo nodded. "Your sister told me. It's a shame about your men."

"Yes, it is. And it's something I can't tolerate. These robberies have to end, and that's why I have a proposition for you, Mr. Fargo."

Fargo had a hunch he knew what the colonel was going to say next, and Drummond didn't surprise him.

"I'd like to hire you to take charge of getting my silver shipments safely from the mine to Las Vegas. I'm aware that you've worked with the army a great deal, so I know I can trust you to take all necessary steps to accomplish your mission."

"It's not my mission yet," Fargo pointed out. "Not until I agree to take the job. And I'm inclined to say thanks, but no, thanks, Colonel."

From the other desk, Lily said, "Oh, but why, Mr. Fargo? I think it's an excellent idea."

"Stay out of this, Lily," Drummond snapped. "This is a business matter."

"Sorry, Henry," she murmured.

Fargo frowned. He didn't care for the way Drummond had spoken to Lily. A fella ought to be nicer than that to his own sister. Not to mention the fact that if Lily was keeping books for her brother, she was already involved in his business.

But he didn't want to get involved in Drummond family squabbles any more than he did in the ones involving Jim McLeod and his daughter Rosa, so he didn't say anything. Drummond leaned forward over the desk and went on. "Listen, Fargo, I'll make it worth your while. I've sunk everything I have into that silver mine, so I can't afford to fail. I can't afford to lose any more men or ore shipments, either. It's already getting difficult to find drivers and guards. I'm sure that with the famous Trailsman taking charge, men will be more likely to want to work for me."

Everything Drummond said made sense, and Fargo

knew the man was in a bind. It was a reasonable offer. Under other circumstances, he might have been tempted to accept it. For one thing, it would mean he'd be spending more time around the very attractive Lily Drummond.

But even though he wasn't exactly flush right now, he wasn't looking for a job, either. The past few months had been rough ones, during which he had been involved in several dangerous, bloody dustups, and he had been drifting southward in hopes of taking life easy for a while. Maybe ride on down to Mexico and spend the winter somewhere warm and sleepy. The idea of swapping lead with a bunch of bandits just didn't appeal to him right now.

"Sorry," he said, shaking his head. "I reckon I'm not the right man for the job."

"But—" Drummond stopped short and sat up straighter in his chair, his back stiffening as if he realized that he was about to beg, and he was too proud a man to do that, no matter what the situation. He gave Fargo a curt nod instead and said, "Very well. I'll respect your decision, sir. But surely you'll allow me to reward you for your services this afternoon."

"That's not necessary."

"I insist."

Seeing that refusing was just going to upset Drummond even more, Fargo said, "Well, if you'd like to buy me a drink later, I could see my way clear to accepting that."

"I'll go you one better. Have dinner with Lily and me tonight. We're staying at the hotel, and they have an adequate dining room there."

Fargo looked around at Lily again. She had gone back to entering figures in the ledger, but he could tell from the way she cocked her head that she was listening and waiting for his answer with some interest.

"That would be fine," he told the colonel. "I'm much obliged."

"No more so than I am for your help." Drummond rose to his feet, and so did Fargo. As they shook hands, Drummond went on. "Seven o'clock, then?"

"I'll be there," Fargo promised. He turned to the railing, opened the gate, and stepped through it. Pausing beside Lily's desk, he told her, "I'll see you later, Miss Drummond."

"Good-bye, Mr. Fargo . . . until this evening."

Fargo put his hat on and left the office, hearing Drummond and Lily talking as he did so. He couldn't make out the words, though, and he wasn't going to stand around and eavesdrop.

He went back to the saloon, untied the Ovaro from the hitch rail, and led the stallion along the street to a small livery stable he had noticed earlier. He paid the elderly hostler for a stall for the next few days, then led the Ovaro in. Once he had unsaddled, grained, and watered the stallion, Fargo strolled back outside. The sun hung low on the western horizon, and the heat of the day had eased slightly. It was still pretty warm, though.

The sound of hoofbeats drew Fargo's attention. He turned his head to look along the street and saw half a dozen riders coming into Las Vegas from the south. All six of them wore sombreros. Four were dressed like vaqueros, in tight trousers and short *charro* jackets. The other two men, who rode in front, wore similar garb, but their clothes were more expensive, made of finer fabrics and decorated with fancy stitching. The big black horses they rode had silver conchos on their harnesses.

One of the men was older, with a weathered face the color of saddle leather and a pointed silvery goatee. The man beside him was younger and clean-shaven. His handsome face had an arrogant cast to it and bore a resemblance to that of the older man. Father and son, Fargo thought as they rode past, or possibly uncle and nephew.

The younger man glared at Fargo with a defiant, challenging expression. The attitude had to be a habit with him, because he had no reason to feel that way. Fargo had never seen him before. He returned the look with a level stare of his own.

The young Mexican moved his hand slightly toward the ivory-handled butt of a Colt holstered on his hip, but the older man spoke sharply to him in a quiet voice. They rode on, backs stiff with stubborn pride that reminded Fargo of the way Drummond had reacted to his refusal of that job.

With a shake of his head, he put the newcomers out of his mind and walked toward the saloon. It would be a while before he was supposed to meet the colonel and Lily at the hotel for dinner, so he thought he might scout out the prospects for a poker game at the Silver Queen Saloon.

He wondered if he would see Rosa McLeod when he went to the hotel later. What were the odds that he would find two such lovely women in a raw little frontier settlement like Las Vegas?

3

Fargo found Jim McLeod in the saloon, nursing a beer as he leaned on the bar. "How did it go with Rosa?" he asked as he came up beside the big mountain man.

"Oh, hell, I don't know," McLeod rumbled. "She claims she ought to come along with me so's she can cook for me and help me with the prospectin', and I said she ought to stay here in town where I know she'd be safe. We didn't come to no agreement."

"Well, I'm sure you'll work it out with her." Fargo told McLeod about his visit to Colonel Drummond's office. "I'm supposed to have dinner with him and his sister a little later at the hotel."

McLeod grinned. "The colonel's sister's a looker, I'll bet. You got a way of attractin' 'em, Skye, just like honey draws flies."

"She's a handsome woman," Fargo admitted as he motioned for the bartender to bring him a beer.

"How come you didn't take the job the colonel offered you? Sounds like the sort o' thing that'd be just right for you."

"I don't know," Fargo said. "Just wasn't in the mood to get shot at by a bunch of bandits again anytime soon, I reckon."

"Hell, if things stayed too peaceful for very long, you'd get plumb bored."

"You may be right about that," Fargo acknowledged

with a chuckle. He took a sip of his beer and turned to put his back against the bar as he looked over the room. "Right now I've got my eye open for a game." He nodded toward one of the tables where a man in a frock coat was playing cards with three other men who appeared to be miners.

"I reckon that tinhorn'll give you one," McLeod agreed. "He'll be in for a surprise if he tries to pull anything slick, though. I never saw anybody who could spot a cheat as good as you, Skye."

"Maybe he's an honest gambler," Fargo suggested.

McLeod grunted as if to comment on what a farfetched possibility *that* was.

Fargo hadn't made arrangements for a place to stay yet, so after chatting with McLeod for a few more minutes, he picked up his saddlebags and the Henry at the livery stable, where he had left them earlier, and walked over to the hotel. It was a flat-roofed, two-story adobe building with a balcony over its front porch. He went inside and rented a room for the next couple of nights, then took his gear upstairs and dropped it off before heading back down to the dining room. It was late enough now for him to meet Colonel Drummond and Lily.

They were already sitting at one of the tables. A bluechecked tablecloth covered it, a bit of luxury in generally no-frills surroundings. Fargo took off his hat as he approached. He had already used it while he was upstairs to knock as much of the dust off his buckskins as he could.

Drummond saw him coming and stood up. Lily smiled a greeting. The colonel shook hands with Fargo and motioned him into one of the empty chairs.

"Good to see you again, Fargo. I don't suppose you've changed your mind about accepting that job I offered you."

"I'm afraid not," Fargo replied with a shake of his head.

Drummond sighed. "Very well. I won't bother you about it again."

"No bother," Fargo said. "Another time, I might have said yes. Right now, though, I'm headed south."

"Are you going to Mexico?" Lily asked. "I've always wanted to visit there."

"I might. Haven't really decided yet."

Drummond grunted. "I saw plenty of Mexico back in 'forty-eight, especially Vera Cruz."

"I've heard it was pretty bad down there," Fargo said.

"Any war is bad. Soldiers know that better than anyone. Sometimes they're necessary, though."

A waiter came over to take their orders; then Fargo said to Drummond, "Tell me about your mine."

Lily spoke up before her brother could reply, saying, "It's called the Lily Belle. Wasn't that sweet of Henry, naming it after me?"

"That's a nice name," Fargo said.

"We're taking out reasonably high-grade ore," Drummond said, "at an acceptable rate of tonnage. I realize that's rather vague. . . ."

Fargo shook his head. "No need to go into details. A man's business is his own. I'm curious, though, what made you leave the army to come out here and prospect."

"I'd had enough of soldiering and wanted something I could call my own for a change. Also, I knew that Lily would be leaving Saint Louis and coming west to join me after our parents passed away, and I wanted something she could be involved with as well."

Lily smiled. "I told you he's sweet."

That wasn't a word Fargo would have applied to the brusque, all-business Henry Drummond, but then he wasn't related to the man, either. He was struck by the similarity in the backgrounds of Lily and Rosa, both of them coming here to Nevada Territory to join relatives.

25

The white-aproned waiter brought their food, and for a while the three of them concentrated on their meal. The steaks were all right, Fargo thought, a little tough but not bad.

While they were eating, the two men Fargo had seen ride into town earlier came into the dining room. They had taken off their sombreros but still wore the expensive clothes. The younger one stopped short as he caught sight of Fargo, but the older one put a hand on his arm, spoke quietly, and urged him on to one of the tables. Their demeanor convinced Fargo more than ever that they were father and son.

Drummond noticed the newcomers, too. "Hmmph," he said. "Strangers in town, and from south of the border, too, I'd say." The dislike was easy to hear in his voice. Since Drummond had helped fight a war against the Mexicans less than fifteen years earlier, Fargo supposed that was understandable, although as far as he was concerned, the past was past and it was always better to look forward than back.

Fargo enjoyed the meal. Lily was very pleasant company, and even Drummond's stiff attitude loosened a bit as the evening went on. Fargo was about to say good night to them and head back over to the saloon to see if there was an empty chair at that poker table, when Rosa Mc-Leod came into the dining room.

Instantly, the young man shot to his feet and cried, "Rosa!" He started toward her. His father reached out and caught hold of his sleeve, but the young man shook him off and rushed across the dining room. Rosa shrank back, her eyes widening in surprise and fear.

"Guillermo!" she said. "What . . . what are you doing here?"

Fargo had put it together in his head as soon as the young man stood up and called Rosa's name. He was

Guillermo Soto, and the older man had to be his father Victorio, Jim McLeod's old enemy. Fargo wasn't surprised that they had tracked Rosa here to Las Vegas.

That meant Guillermo had been among the men Fargo and McLeod had battled with in that shadowy Santa Fe alley a couple of years earlier. Fargo hadn't recognized him, but from the way Guillermo had been glaring at him, the young man must have gotten a better look at him during the ruckus and recalled him from that incident. That would explain Guillermo's hostility.

Rosa turned to leave the dining room, but Guillermo grabbed her shoulders and twisted her around to face him again. Fargo could tell from the way Rosa's face contorted that Guillermo's fingers were digging painfully into her flesh.

"Excuse me," he murmured to Drummond and Lily as he came to his feet.

"Are you going to get involved in that, Fargo?" the colonel asked, disapproval in his voice. "It seems like more of a private matter."

"No offense, Colonel, but so was that attack on your wagons this afternoon, and I took cards in that game. Besides, I know the young lady."

He didn't waste time on further explanations. Instead he strode across the dining room toward Guillermo and Rosa. The young man held her tightly as she tried to pull away.

"You must come back to Santa Fe with me," he said. "I have followed you all the way here."

"I told you to leave me alone, Señor Soto!" Rosa gasped. "I want nothing to do with you."

"Your father has poisoned you against me with his lies—"

"It is your father who is the liar!" Rosa shot back. "He has always hated my father!"

"With good reason! But I love you, Rosa—"

Fargo's hand fell on Guillermo's shoulder. "Let the young lady go," he said. "I don't reckon she cares for your company."

Guillermo swung around sharply, anger darkening his face. He struck Fargo's hand aside. "How dare you touch me, gringo?" he demanded. He reached for the gun on his hip. "I'll—"

The fingers of Fargo's left hand closed around Guillermo's wrist. He clamped down hard enough that bones grated together. The young man gasped in pain as the fingers of his gun hand involuntarily splayed out, unable to grasp the butt of his revolver.

Fargo looked over Guillermo's shoulder and said, "Rosa, get out of here. Don't worry. Nobody's going to bother you."

Behind Fargo, the metallic ratcheting of a gun being cocked punctuated a harsh command. "Unhand my son, señor, or I will be forced to shoot you."

Fargo glanced back and saw Victorio Soto pointing a heavy old cap-and-ball pistol at him. From the corner of his eye, Fargo spotted Colonel Drummond rising to his feet as well. The colonel aimed his Colt at Soto and said, "Drop that gun, mister, right now."

Everyone else in the dining room sat in tense silence, waiting to see what was going to happen. Fargo knew that the room had become like a powder keg—all it needed was the tiniest spark to make it blow all to hell.

Now free from Guillermo's grip, Rosa turned and rushed out of the dining room. Fargo let go of the young man's wrist. Guillermo stumbled back a step and cradled his right wrist in his left hand. Fargo could see him struggling to keep tears of pain from rolling down his cheeks.

Slowly, so that he wouldn't spook either of them into pulling the trigger, Fargo turned toward Soto and Drummond. "It's over," he told them when he was facing them. "Pouch those irons."

"You have insulted my son's pride," Soto said, his voice stiff with outrage.

"He'll get over it," Fargo snapped.

The old man's gaze flicked past him, and that was all the warning the Trailsman needed. Fargo twisted aside, and the blade that Guillermo had just tried to drive into his back missed narrowly. Fargo didn't know where the youngster had gotten the knife—it was probably hidden somewhere under his clothes—and he didn't care. He brought the edge of his hand down on Guillermo's wrist in a sharp blow that made the knife clatter to the floor.

Guillermo lunged at him. Fargo kept turning, pivoting so that most of his weight was behind the right fist he hooked into Guillermo's jaw. The punch landed with the sound of an ax biting deep into a block of firewood on a frosty morning. Guillermo's head slew to one side under the impact. At the same time, Fargo kicked his legs out from under him. Guillermo crashed to the floor.

Fargo halfway expected shots to ring out from Soto and Drummond, but the tense silence continued. A rush of feet broke it a few seconds later. The four vaqueros who had accompanied the Sotos into town charged into the dining room. Fargo didn't know if the old man had managed to summon them in some way, or if they had heard the commotion and just figured that Guillermo would be in the middle of it. Either way, they were here, and as they spotted Guillermo lying senseless on the floor at Fargo's feet, they shouted angry curses in Spanish and rushed him.

Fargo could have palmed out the revolver on his hip, but he worried that drawing his gun would be the spark needed to ignite the conflagration. Instead, he reached lower and pulled the Arkansas toothpick from the sheath strapped to his calf. The men paused warily as they saw lamplight glint from the knife's long, heavy blade.

"Back off, hombres," Fargo warned them. "I don't want to hurt anybody."

They might have thought twice about rushing him, but at that moment, Guillermo regained his senses enough to tackle Fargo from behind. Lily Drummond shouted a warning to him, but it came too late. Fargo lost his balance and went down, falling heavily. The four vaqueros swarmed over him. One of them kicked the knife out of his hand.

Booted feet thudded into Fargo's ribs and rocked him back and forth. He reached up, grabbed a foot, and heaved on it as hard as he could. The man it belonged to went over backward with a startled yell. That gave Fargo a little breathing room. He rolled out of the way of another kick and tackled a second man. Fargo planted a knee in the man's belly, then scrambled to his feet.

He was surrounded. Fists thudded into him, but he dealt out punishment in return, bruising his knuckles on the faces of Soto's men. But despite his best efforts, he was still outnumbered five to one, and it was only a matter of time before he went down again. Once he did, they would probably stomp him within an inch of his life.

It didn't come to that, because suddenly, with a roar like that of a charging grizzly, Jim McLeod entered the fray. The massive mountain man charged into the knot of struggling men from the dining room entrance and flung two of the vaqueros aside. They crashed into the wall like rag dolls thrown by a petulant child. The fingers of McLeod's hamlike hands closed around the necks of the other two vaqueros and brought their skulls together with a resounding crack.

That left Fargo facing a suddenly alone and desperate Guillermo. The young man threw several wild punches.

Fargo blocked some of them and avoided the others as he bored in. He hooked a left into Guillermo's midsection that bent the youngster forward and put him in perfect position for the right cross that Fargo sent whistling in. Guillermo went down again, and this time he looked like he wouldn't be moving again for a good long while.

McLeod and Soto glared at each other across the dining room, each of them exclaiming, "You!" at the same time. Soto swung the barrel of his gun toward his old enemy.

Fargo moved fast, stepping over to Soto and grabbing the gun. He shoved it down as Soto fired. The blast was painfully loud in the dining room as the old cap-and-ball pistol roared, but the heavy lead ball thudded harmlessly into the floor. Fargo twisted the gun out of Soto's hand and at the same time motioned for Drummond to lower his weapon.

McLeod started across the room toward Soto, bellowing, "I'm gonna wring your scrawny neck, you bastard! You ain't given me a minute's peace in twenty-five years!"

Fargo got between them. It wouldn't help matters for McLeod to start brawling with Soto, and for another thing, the mountain man was twice the size of the old Mexican. Holding Soto's pistol in one hand, Fargo used his other hand to grab McLeod's shoulder.

"Hold it, Jim," he said. "It's all over."

"It ain't never gonna be over," McLeod insisted. "Not as long as me and him are both still alive."

"Let him go, señor," Soto said. "I do not fear him. He is big, but full of hot air."

"Hot air, is it?" McLeod roared. "I'll show you hot air, you old buzzard!"

Rosa hurried into the dining room. Fargo figured she had gone looking for her father when she rushed out several minutes earlier. "Papa," she said. "Stop it. There's been enough fighting."

McLeod looked like he wanted to shrug Fargo's hand off his shoulder and go after Soto anyway, but his daughter's words held him back. He said, "Blast it, girl—"

"Enough!" Rosa said again. She caught hold of his arm and tugged him toward the door. "Come on. Let's get out of here."

Fargo let go of McLeod as the mountain man reluctantly turned away. McLeod looked back at Soto and said, "Why don't you just go away and leave us alone? Madelina's dead and buried. Let her rest in peace."

"How can I, when you ruined her life?" Soto demanded with a sneer. For a second, Fargo saw the same sort of arrogance on the face of the father that was so prevalent on the face of the son.

Rosa kept pulling on McLeod's arm, but McLeod wasn't going easily. "She was happy with me," he yelled at Soto. "Happier'n she ever would've been with you, you dried-up pelican!"

Rosa was just about to maneuver her father out of the dining room when another man appeared in the entrance. He was a stockily built, dark-faced gent with a heavy black mustache. "Mr. Everett!" Rosa said as the man blocked their path.

"I heard there's trouble in here," the man said. "Who's responsible for it?"

"They are," Soto snapped as he pointed at Rosa and McLeod. "And this barbarian," he added with a wave of his hand at Fargo.

"I won't have brawls in my hotel over a servant," Everett snapped as he glared at Rosa. "Get your things and get out. You're through here."

"Now wait just a da—I mean, a doggoned minute," McLeod protested. "My gal ain't to blame for anything that happened here. It was all that varmint Soto's fault, him and that wolf cub o' his."

Colonel Drummond stepped up to the tense group, saying, "Mr. McLeod is correct, sir. The young man there instigated the disturbance." He nodded toward Guillermo Soto, who was coming around and being helped to his feet by the two vaqueros who hadn't been knocked out cold during the ruckus.

Everett rubbed his jaw and scowled. As a hotel keeper, he wanted to side with his guests, but in this case he had the Sotos on one side and Fargo and Drummond on the other, and all of them were staying here.

In the end, he didn't come down on either side. He just said, "Rosa, go to your room and try to avoid Señor Soto and his son while they're staying here."

"That ain't fair," McLeod said. "Rosa ain't to blame for nothin'."

"Be that as it may, evidently her presence provoked the fight."

"Hell with this." McLeod grabbed Rosa's hand. "I ain't lettin' no fancy-pants hotel man talk to you like that. You ain't workin' here no more."

"But, Papa, what will I do?" she asked. "Where will I stay?"

Colonel Drummond cleared his throat. "If I might, ah, offer a suggestion . . . ?"

McLeod looked at him. "I'm listenin', Colonel."

"You may or may not be aware that I offered Mr. Fargo the job of getting my silver shipments safely to town," Drummond said. "He declined. So now I'm offering the job to you, Mr. McLeod."

"Playin' second fiddle to Skye Fargo, eh?" McLeod frowned darkly for a moment, then laughed. "I don't reckon I can complain about that, knowin' the sort o' fella he is."

"And that's not all," Drummond went on. "I can offer employment to your daughter as well. Miss McLeod can stay out at the mine headquarters. I really need someone to do the cooking and put the place in better shape."

Hope appeared on Rosa's face. "I could do that," she said to her father.

McLeod frowned again. "Are you sure you'd want to take a job like that, honey?"

"It's better than what I was doing here!"

Everett scowled at that, but Rosa ignored him.

"And we would be together much of the time," she went on to McLeod.

He scratched at his bushy beard and nodded slowly. "Yeah, maybe it ain't a bad idea. I figured on doin' some prospectin' of my own—"

"You still can," Drummond put in. "There'll be plenty of times when your services aren't needed, and you'll be free then to do as you please, even if that includes looking for other veins of silver. It's really an excellent solution to your dilemma, if I do say so myself."

"I reckon maybe you're right." McLeod looked at Fargo. "What do you think, Skye?"

"I think it's up to you," Fargo said.

Guillermo Soto picked that moment to plead in a ragged voice, "Don't listen to any of them, Rosa. Come back to Santa Fe with me!"

That must have helped McLeod to make up his mind, because he stuck out a paw and said to Drummond, "You got a deal, Colonel."

Drummond smiled and shook his hand. "Excellent! The two of you can ride out to the mine with me tomorrow. I'll be taking all three wagons back."

"In the meantime," Fargo said to Rosa, "you can have my room here in the hotel for the night."

"But where will you stay, Señor Fargo?" she asked.

"There's a livery stable right down the street," Fargo

replied with a grin. "I reckon if that horse of mine can stand me for the night, I can stand him."

Guillermo took a step toward them and began, "Rosa—" but his father caught hold of his arm.

"Come, my son," the old man grated. "Our trip here was wasted. We will return to Santa Fe."

"But, Father, I cannot abandon my love!"

Soto slapped Guillermo across the face. "Have you no pride? Pursuing a woman is one thing. Humiliating yourself is another! We are done here!"

He stalked out of the dining room, practically dragging Guillermo with him. The two vaqueros helped their semiconscious brethren follow their employers.

Everett said to Drummond, "I'm sorry about this disturbance, Colonel. My apologies to your sister as well. I regret that she had to witness such violence."

"At least there was no real bloodshed," Drummond said.

With a sigh, Everett said, "I'm not sure this settlement will ever amount to anything."

"Give it time," Drummond suggested. "Every civilization has its growing pains."

McLeod said to Fargo, "We'll go gather up Rosa's gear and take it up to your room, if you're sure about lettin' her use it tonight."

"I'm sure," Fargo said. He gave the key to McLeod. "Where are you staying, Jim?"

"I'll be sharin' a stall down at the stable with my hoss, just like you, Skye."

The McLeods left the dining room. Fargo brushed himself off as he and Drummond walked back to the table where Lily sat waiting for them. "Sorry about the ruckus," Fargo told her as he and the colonel sat down.

"There's no need to apologize," she said. "You did the

only thing you could. If I were a man, I would have stepped in to help that poor girl, too."

"What's the story there?" Drummond asked.

Fargo didn't care much for gossiping, but he figured that Drummond and Lily deserved an explanation, considering all that they had seen for themselves already. He told them about the long-standing grudge between Jim McLeod and Victorio Soto, as well as Guillermo Soto's pursuit of Rosa that had just aggravated the situation.

"How tragic, that the old man never got over his lost love," Lily murmured when Fargo was finished.

"Yes, but he didn't have to allow that loss to poison not only his own life but that of his son as well," her brother said. "Perhaps now it's finally over. Señor Soto said that he and his son are going back to Santa Fe."

"I hope that's the way it turns out," Fargo said as he reached for one of the cups of coffee that the waiter had brought to the table. "It sure would make things simpler for Jim and Rosa."

But as he sipped the strong black brew, he wondered if Soto was truly abandoning his quest for vengeance on Jim McLeod for what happened so long ago.

He wouldn't bet a hat on it, Fargo decided.

4

After finishing the interrupted meal, Fargo thanked Colonel Drummond and said good night to him and Lily. He stood up to leave and shook hands with Drummond; then Lily surprised him a little by extending her hand, too. Fargo took it and enjoyed the feel of her smooth, warm flesh. The firm grip of Lily's slender fingers possessed quite a bit of strength. Fargo enjoyed that, too.

"Good night, Mr. Fargo," she told him. "I hope we see you again while you're here in Las Vegas."

"That's possible. I'm not really sure when I'll be riding on."

"I'll be heading back to the mine tomorrow for a few days, so you may be gone by the time I get back," Drummond said. "Lily will be here in the settlement, though. If you need anything, don't hesitate to call on her. As far as I'm concerned, we still owe you a debt of gratitude for helping save that ore shipment this afternoon. One meal hardly squares accounts."

"Maybe not, but the pleasant company does," Fargo said. "So long, Colonel, and good luck."

He went upstairs to his room, thinking that he'd get his gear and fetch it down to the livery stable before he wandered over to the saloon and spent a couple of hours playing poker. Thinking that McLeod and Rosa might still be in the room, he paused in front of the door and rapped on it.

Rosa's voice came from inside. "Who's there?"

"Just me," Fargo said. "Thought I'd get my saddlebags and rifle."

"Come in."

Fargo twisted the knob, swung the door open, and stepped inside. He stopped short at the sight of Rosa standing there next to the bed in a thin cotton shift. The large dark circles of the nipples that crowned her high, firm breasts were clearly visible through the fabric, as was the triangle of hair at the juncture of her thighs.

Fargo's jaw tightened. "That's not really the proper way to dress when you invite an hombre into your room," he told her.

Rosa smiled and said, "Or perhaps it's exactly the proper way to dress, depending on what you intend to do."

"Your pa and I are old friends," Fargo said as he shook his head. "This isn't right, Rosa, and it's not going to happen."

She took a step toward him and lifted a hand. "Why not, Skye? You're being kind enough to give me your hotel room for the night—"

"And I don't expect anything in return," Fargo said.

"Expecting something and having it offered freely to you are two different things."

"Where's Jim?"

"He's already gone back to the stable. You don't have to worry about him catching us, if that's what you're thinking."

"That's not what I'm worried about," Fargo said. "I'm worried about taking advantage of a young woman."

"I'm not some blushing virgin, so you don't have to worry about that, Skye," she snapped. "I haven't been for quite some time. And before you ask, no, my father doesn't know about that. It's none of his business."

Fargo couldn't argue with that, but neither could he bring himself to do something he knew his old friend would regard as a betrayal. He stepped around Rosa and started toward his saddlebags, which were hung over the foot of the bedstead. The Henry rifle was propped in the corner.

Rosa moved closer to him, and her arms went around his neck. Fargo felt the heat of her body through the shift as she pressed herself against him.

"Please, Skye," she whispered. "Things have been . . . terrible. First in Santa Fe, with Guillermo always after me, and then here in Las Vegas. That man Everett seems to think that just because I worked for him, it gave him certain . . . privileges. . . ."

Her voice trailed off as a shudder went through her. Fargo's jaw clenched, and he wondered if he ought to have a word with the hotel keeper.

"I just need someone to hold me," Rosa went on. "Just for a little while."

Fargo felt the warmth of her breath on his face, saw the way her breasts rose and fell as they molded themselves to his chest, smelled the honeyed fragrance of her thick, dark hair. His manhood hardened against the softness of her belly, and he knew that if he wound up in bed with Rosa McLeod, it wouldn't be just to hold her. It would be much more than that, and she was bound to know that, too.

"Sorry," he said, and he had seldom been more sincere in expressing that emotion. He wanted to make love to Rosa. She wanted it, too, and the only thing stopping them from winding up in that bed was Fargo's refusal to go against his sense of honor.

Having a conscience and a code was damned inconvenient at times, he told himself, not to mention frustrating.

Despite that frustration, he reached up, grasped Rosa's wrists, and took her arms from around his neck. As she watched him with disbelief on her lovely face, he picked up his saddlebags and rifle and turned toward the door.

"Skye . . ."

"I know," he said. "I'm being a damned fool. But sometimes a man doesn't have any choice in the matter."

He stepped out into the hallway and eased the door closed behind him. Faintly, he heard angry muttering in Spanish on the other side of the panel, and a smile touched his lips.

Yeah, he reflected, definitely a damned fool.

Fargo finally made it to the Silver Queen Saloon for that poker game. The gambler he had seen in the saloon earlier in the day welcomed him to the table.

"You probably don't remember me, Fargo," the frock-coated man said, "but we played in the same game for a couple of hours in Wichita, about three years ago."

"At Jack Ferguson's place?" Fargo asked.

"That's right."

A smile creased the Trailsman's bearded face. "I remember you. Kelly, isn't it?"

"That's right." The gambler reached across the table to shake hands. "Thad Kelly."

One of the other players, a burly miner, glared. "You two gents are awful chummy," he said. "You ain't plannin' on workin' together in this game, are you?"

Fargo's eyes narrowed in irritation. Before he could say anything, though, Kelly snapped, "If that's the way you feel, friend, maybe you'd better just pick up your money and leave. I run an honest game."

Fargo remembered from Wichita that that claim was true. Kelly was a good enough poker player to win consistently without cheating. Fargo didn't appreciate the miner's implication, either, and his dark eyes glittered dangerously.

"Sorry," the miner muttered. "Didn't mean no offense, Kelly."

"That's all right." The gambler began shuffling the deck. "Let's play, gentlemen."

The next two hours were a hard-fought battle, with either Fargo or Kelly winning nearly every hand. At the end of that time, Fargo was ahead, but only by about twenty dollars. The day had been long enough, though, that he stifled a yawn and said at the end of a hand, "I reckon that's about enough for me."

"You're not going to give me a chance to win my money back?" Kelly asked.

Fargo grinned. "That old dodge isn't going to work on me, Thad. You ought to know better."

"Yeah, I reckon I ought to," Kelly said with a chuckle. "Good night, then, Skye."

The miner who had been suspicious earlier had stayed in the game, losing steadily even though the bets he made were small. He was almost out of money, so he said with a bitter edge in his voice, "I'm near busted. I might as well quit, too."

Fargo and Kelly ignored him. The gambler said, "How about a drink before you go, Skye?"

Fargo thought it over for a second and then nodded. "Sounds good. I'm buying, though, since I won more than you did."

"I won't argue with you."

The two of them stood up and went to the bar while the miner gathered up his few coins and stalked out of the saloon. Fargo and Kelly chatted idly for a few minutes as they sipped from glasses of whiskey, reminiscing about places they had been and people they knew. Then Fargo threw back what was left of his drink and said, "Good night, Thad."

Fargo left the Silver Queen and started toward the stable where he'd be sharing a stall with the Ovaro tonight. As always, he took a quick look around the street, searching for any sign of trouble. Caution was a long-standing habit with him.

Not seeing anything that set off warning bells, Fargo walked on, but he had taken only a few steps toward the stable when the hair on the back of his neck suddenly prickled. Instinct and keen senses combined to warn him. He heard boot leather scuff against the ground behind him, the noise so faint that most men never would have noticed it.

But Skye Fargo wasn't most men—and that was the reason he was still alive.

His hand flashed to his gun as he suddenly lunged to one side and whirled around. Even as he moved, Colt flame blossomed redly in the stygian darkness of an alley mouth on the other side of the saloon. Fargo palmed out his own revolver, thumbing back the hammer as the barrel came up. The gun bucked in his hand as flame belched from its muzzle.

Another orange flash stabbed back at him. A bullet sang past his ear. Fargo drew back the hammer of his Colt and was about to fire again when the saloon door burst open and a figure leaped out into the street.

A third shot came from the bushwhacker's gun. In the light that spilled through the open doorway, Fargo saw Thad Kelly's face contort in pain. The gambler's back arched as he stumbled forward a couple of steps. Then Kelly fell to his knees.

Fargo hurried toward the alley at an angle so that Kelly wouldn't be in the line of fire. He thumbed off two more shots as he ran. Then he reached Kelly's side and holstered the gun as he bent to catch Kelly under the arms. Fargo hefted the gambler and hauled him back into the saloon, which had erupted into confusion because of the shots.

"Kelly's hit," Fargo said. "Somebody look after him."

Then he wheeled around and dashed out the door again. He pressed his back against the wall of the saloon and watched the alley mouth, holding his Colt ready for instant use.

When no more shots sounded and he didn't hear anyone moving around the alley, Fargo edged forward. With his free hand, he fished a lucifer out of a pocket in his buckskin shirt and snapped it into life with his thumbnail. He tossed the flaming match into the alley mouth.

The lucifer didn't draw any more shots. Fargo twisted around the corner in a crouch, the gun in his hand leveled as he swept it from side to side. The flickering light from the match revealed that the alley was empty now. Fargo looked at the sandy ground, hoping to see some dark splashes of blood, but there weren't any. Evidently, none of his shots had found its target.

Convinced that whoever had ambushed him had fled, Fargo turned and went back to the entrance of the Silver Queen. When he stepped into the saloon, he didn't like the hushed silence that hung over the room. He looked at the bar and saw that the patrons had lifted Thad Kelly onto the hardwood.

Kelly's right arm hung limp in front of the bar. Fargo stepped over to him and looked down into a pale, lifeless face. Kelly's eyes were still open and staring at the ceiling, but they didn't see anything.

With a grim expression on his face and a bitter-sour taste under his tongue, Fargo gently closed Kelly's eyes. He looked around at the men who had gathered in front of the bar, and one of them who wore a brown tweed suit said, "There wasn't a thing we could do for him, mister. He didn't live ten seconds after you brought him in here. We would have helped him if we could, you have my word on that. My name's Sawtell, and I own this place. Kelly was well liked."

Not by everybody, thought Fargo. That miner who had left a short time earlier hadn't been happy about the way the game had gone this evening. He had seemed to be holding a grudge against both Fargo and Kelly. It was possible he had waited around in the alley until Fargo came out, then started taking potshots at him. Kelly had just had the bad luck to get in the way of one of those slugs.

But the sore loser wasn't the only one who could have decided to ambush him, Fargo reminded himself. Guillermo Soto had been mighty upset earlier at the hotel, and Fargo wouldn't put a little bushwhacking past the arrogant young bravo.

For that matter, several members of the gang that had jumped Colonel Drummond's ore wagons that afternoon had survived the ruckus. They could have followed Fargo and McLeod into town. It was entirely possible that the outlaws drifted in and out of Las Vegas, pretending to be honest citizens.

Those thoughts flashed through Fargo's head in a matter of seconds. As they did, Sawtell, the saloonkeeper, went on. "What happened out there?"

"Somebody ambushed me," Fargo said. "Kelly came out to see what was going on and walked right into a bushwhacker's bullet."

One of the saloon's customers said, "When the shooting started, I heard him say that he was afraid somebody had thrown down on you, mister. He rushed out to help you."

"And it got him killed," Fargo said with a grim nod.

Sawtell asked, "Did you get a good look at whoever was doing the shooting?"

"I didn't get any kind of look," Fargo replied. "It was too dark to see anything in that alley, and he took off for the tall and uncut when his first shot missed and I put up a fight." Fargo started reloading the expended chambers in his Colt. "Is there any sort of law in these parts?"

"Las Vegas is too young for that," Sawtell said. "There's been some talk about hiring a marshal, but nobody's gotten around to doing anything yet except talking. I suppose there's a county sheriff somewhere who has jurisdiction, but I don't even know where the county seat is."

Neither did Fargo, and he didn't suppose it mattered. Like most Westerners, the citizens of this raw young settlement handled their own problems, and it was obvious to everyone in the Silver Queen what had happened. Thad Kelly had met his death through bad luck and the villainy of an unknown bushwhacker.

"We do have an undertaker," Sawtell went on. "He's getting a lot of business these days."

That was always the way, Fargo reflected grimly. Wherever he went, there was always more business for the undertaker.

As soon as it was light enough to see the next morning, Fargo checked out the alley and the area behind the saloon. Jim McLeod accompanied him. When Fargo had gotten to the livery stable the night before, he'd told the old mountain man about the ambush.

"Yeah, I heard the shots," McLeod had said. "Didn't think much of 'em, though. Somebody's always firin' off pistols in town. Any town."

Now the keen eyes of both men searched the ground for clues to the bushwhacker's identity. Fargo saw plenty of footprints—too many to be of any use, in fact. The tracks were a muddled mess. He noted one thing that might be helpful, however. There were no hoofprints. Nobody had ridden a horse back here recently, which meant that the bushwhacker had either left Las Vegas on foot. . . .

Or was still here.

"If you stay around these parts long enough, maybe you can come out to that mine o' the colonel's and pay me and Rosa a visit," McLeod suggested as they walked toward the hotel.

"I might just do that," Fargo said. He hadn't told McLeod about what had happened in the hotel room between him and Rosa, and he wasn't going to. When you got right down to it, Fargo told himself, nothing all that bad had taken place.

He suppressed the sigh he felt coming on as that thought went through his head.

"Come in," Rosa called when McLeod knocked on the door. She didn't ask who it was, which led Fargo to hope that she would actually be dressed this time.

She was, in a dark blue dress that hugged her ripe body in appealing ways. She smiled at her father, then gave Fargo a cool look. If McLeod noticed, he didn't say anything.

"Ready to go, darlin'?" he asked.

"I am," Rosa said. She gestured toward a small bag on the bed. "I don't have much."

"One o' these days when I strike it rich, you'll have all the geegaws and furbelows any gal could ever want," McLeod promised. "You got my word on that."

Rosa laughed. "I'm just glad to be with you, Papa. Right now, that's all I want."

The three of them went downstairs to the lobby. Everett, the hotel's proprietor, stood behind the desk now. Remembering what Rosa had told him the night before about the liberties the man had attempted to take with her, Fargo gave him a narrow-eyed look that made Everett swallow hard. He probably had a pretty good idea what it was about.

As they emerged from the hotel, Fargo looked down the street and saw the three ore wagons lined up in front of the mining company office. The wagons were empty now, except for some supplies that Drummond was taking back out to the mine for his men. The hired drivers were already on two of the wagons. Drummond and Lily stood beside the first one.

"Good morning," Drummond greeted Fargo, McLeod, and Rosa as they walked up. "Are you ready to go, Miss McLeod?"

"I am," Rosa replied. "I'm looking forward to it."

"I must say, it will be nice to have a feminine touch around the place for a change," Drummond said.

"Henry!" Lily scolded. "You know I would have come out to the mine any time you wanted me to."

He patted her shoulder. "You're much too valuable to me here, my dear. Someone has to keep track of all the numbers, and you're much better at that than I am."

"Well, just remember, I'm capable of other things, too."

"I'm sure you are." Drummond turned to Fargo. "You haven't changed your mind about coming with us, have you, Mr. Fargo?"

"Nope, the job belongs to Jim," Fargo said as he clapped a hand on McLeod's shoulder. "I'm sure he'll do just fine at it, too."

McLeod hefted the Sharps he carried. "Any varmint tries to lay a finger on your silver, Colonel, he'll get a mighty hole blowed through him by this Big Fifty o' mine."

"Well, let's hope it doesn't come to that again, shall

we?" Drummond said. "My hope is that once word gets around that I have a man of your caliber guarding my ore shipments, the outlaws will stop trying to rob them."

McLeod guffawed. "A man o' my caliber, eh? Like I said, Big Fifty!"

He took Rosa's bag and placed it in the back of the first wagon, then helped her climb to the seat. "I'll go get my horse, Colonel," he told Drummond, "and then I'll be ready to ride."

While McLeod was gone to the livery stable, Drummond gave Lily a somewhat stiff embrace and said, "I'll see you the next time I'm in town, my dear. As always, I worry about leaving you here in this . . . this primitive community."

"I'll be fine, Henry," she assured him. "I never go anywhere except the office and the hotel, and nothing's going to happen to me in either of those places, especially in broad daylight."

"Well, be careful, anyway. This isn't Saint Louis, you know."

"No, it's not . . . and I'm not sure but what it's not safer than Saint Louis."

McLeod came trotting up on his horse a moment later. Drummond climbed onto the seat next to Rosa, and the mountain man asked him, "Roll the wagons, Colonel?"

"Roll the wagons, Mr. McLeod," Drummond said.

Lifting a powerful arm above his head, McLeod swept it forward and called, "Wagons . . . *ho!*", as if he were guiding a hundred prairie schooners full of immigrants bound for the Promised Land, instead of three empty ore wagons. The drivers, including Colonel Drummond, slapped the backs of their teams with the reins and called out to the mules. The balky creatures started forward, and the vehicles lurched into motion behind them.

Fargo and Lily stood there, watching them go. Without

looking at him, Lily asked, "What are your plans now, Mr. Fargo?"

"I don't reckon I have any," Fargo answered honestly.

"Good. Then you won't mind having dinner with me again tonight."

A smile curved Fargo's lips. "No," he said, "I don't reckon I'd mind that at all."

5

Fargo spent most of the morning looking around Las Vegas—not that there was much to see in the still-young town. But he was interested to discover that Victorio and Guillermo Soto were still staying at the hotel, along with their vaqueros. The old man had said they were leaving Las Vegas, but they didn't seem to be in any hurry to do so.

Fargo wondered where Guillermo had been the night before, when those shots had rung out from the alley beside the Silver Queen and cut down Thad Kelly.

He also asked around about the miner who had been upset about losing most of his money in the poker game. The man's name was Duffy, Fargo learned, and no one had seen him around the settlement since the previous night. He had a small claim southwest of Las Vegas that had been stingy in giving up any silver.

Fargo decided to take a ride out there. The Ovaro would probably be glad of the excuse to stretch his legs. The stallion didn't like being cooped up in a stable, even for a day or two.

After lunch, Fargo saddled the Ovaro and rode down the broad valley of the Colorado River. To the west, the mountains in whose foothills Colonel Drummond's mine was located curved closer to the stream. Fargo found Duffy's claim backed up to a ridge several miles southwest of the settlement.

The miner's cabin was just a crude shack. Duffy had

hacked out a tunnel in the ridge face. The dark opening looked like the maw of a hungry animal, Fargo thought as he approached.

He saw a mule tied up next to the shack. The animal brayed at him. Fargo reined in and frowned as he noticed that the mule's water bucket was dry. In this heat, that wasn't good. Duffy neglected his mule, which was one more reason to dislike the man.

"Hey, Duffy!" Fargo called. "Hello, the cabin! Anybody home?"

The Trailsman's voice echoed back at him from the ridge. That was the only answer he received.

"Duffy! You in the mine?"

Still nothing. Fargo swung down from the saddle and dropped the reins. He had trained the Ovaro to remain ground-hitched for as long as necessary.

Fargo picked up the water bucket and looked around for a spring or some other way to fill it. He didn't see anything of the sort, but when he checked a large barrel next to the shack, he found it half full of water. Duffy must have water delivered out here from the springs at Las Vegas, Fargo thought. That would be an expensive proposition for a man whose mine wasn't producing much color.

He moved aside the barrel lid enough to be able to dip the bucket in the water. When he set the bucket on the ground near the mule, the animal dipped his muzzle in it and drank thirstily. Fargo hadn't put enough water in the bucket to cause the mule to founder, even if the critter drank all of it, so he didn't worry about that as he stepped over to the Ovaro and pulled the Henry rifle from its sheath.

Fargo had other worries now.

He levered a round into the Henry's chamber, then started toward the mine tunnel. His keen eyes narrowed as they searched for any sign of movement inside the dark opening in the ridge. He cradled the rifle in his hands, ready to fire at the slightest warning of trouble.

"Duffy!" Fargo called again as he neared the tunnel. "If you're in there, Duffy, sing out!"

Only silence came from the mine.

Knowing that the sunlight would cast him in silhouette as he entered the tunnel, Fargo went in quickly and pressed his back to the rocky wall as soon as he was inside the mine. Duffy had shored up the roof with thick timbers. Fargo used one of them for cover, even though it wasn't thick enough to provide much of a shield from a bullet.

The mine was dead quiet. Not wanting to shout now that he was inside, Fargo lowered his voice and said, "Duffy?" The word echoed faintly.

Fargo's eyes adjusted to the dimness. He saw that the tunnel appeared to be blocked several yards ahead of him. Holding the rifle with one hand, he dug out a match with the other and scraped the lucifer into flame against the wall. Narrowing his eyes against the sudden glare, he saw that the roof of the tunnel had collapsed, forming a large mound of rubble.

A pair of legs clad in rough denim trousers extended from that rubble.

Fargo heaved a sigh as he lowered the rifle. He had figured something was wrong when Duffy didn't answer his hails. This grim discovery explained the silence, as well as the mule's empty water bucket. From the way the dust of the cave-in had already settled, the roof collapse must have happened early this morning, maybe when Duffy entered the tunnel for the first time today.

Fargo walked out of the mine and slid the Henry back in its sheath. He found a lantern in the squalid little shack and carried it back to the tunnel. He lit it and hung it on a peg that Duffy had driven into the wall for that purpose, then started moving the rocks that had crushed the life out of the prospector. Even though he suspected that Duffy might be responsible for Thad Kelly's death, Fargo didn't have it in him to just ride off and leave him here for the scavengers.

Digging out the body was hard work, and Fargo soon broke a sweat. He took off his hat and buckskin shirt and labored stripped to the waist. Eventually he had moved aside enough of the rocks and cleared away enough of the dirt and gravel to grasp Duffy's legs and pull the rest of the body free. It wasn't a pretty sight. The cave-in had crushed Duffy's torso into something barely recognizable as human.

Fargo went back to the shack, stripped the stained and stinking blanket off the bunk, and carried it out to the mine. He wrapped the corpse in it and found some rope to cinch the makeshift shroud tight. Then he carried the body out into the sunlight.

The mule didn't want anything to do with the corpse. Fargo had to struggle to get the body draped across the mule's back and lashed into place, but finally, he got the grim task done. Then he pulled on his shirt, settled his hat on his head, and mounted up. He started back toward Las Vegas on the Ovaro, leading the mule behind them with its burden.

Duffy probably would have denied ambushing him the night before, Fargo thought, but this accident had made it impossible to know for sure if he had been responsible for Kelly's death. That was a stroke of bad luck.

Unless, of course, you were the local undertaker.

Even in a rough-and-tumble young settlement like Las Vegas, the sight of Fargo leading the corpse-laden mule down the street drew quite a bit of attention. Several men walked out to greet him and ask what had happened.

Fargo spotted the Sotos, father and son, standing on the

porch of the hotel. He could have been mistaken, but he thought he saw a look of smug satisfaction on Guillermo's face as he led the mule past them.

A frown creased Fargo's forehead as he thought about that. Duffy was one of the leading suspects in the ambush, and now that he was dead, his guilt couldn't be either confirmed or disproved. Was Guillermo Soto devious enough in his thinking to believe that killing Duffy would reduce the suspicion directed at him?

The damage done to the miner's body by the cave-in was so great that it would be impossible to tell if he had any other wounds. Someone could have snuck into the mine, gunned down Duffy, then brought the tunnel roof down on top of him.

The idea was far-fetched, Fargo decided, but not impossible.

He reined to a stop in front of the undertaking parlor. The undertaker, a graying, solemn-faced hombre, must have heard the commotion in the street. He came out to greet Fargo and nodded toward the blanket-wrapped shape.

"Who's that?"

"A miner named Duffy," Fargo replied.

"I know the man," the undertaker said with a nod. "Did you kill him, Mr. Fargo?"

"Nope. He got caught in a cave-in. The roof of his mine tunnel collapsed."

"That's terrible. I assume the casket will be closed for whatever services are held."

"That'd be a good idea," Fargo said. "I'll give you a hand with him."

They unloaded the body from the mule and carried it into the building. As they came out again, Fargo went on. "I don't know if Duffy had any money. I'll take care of the cost of the burial if he didn't."

That offer brought a surprised frown to the undertaker's face. "I understood there was some bad blood between the two of you. I heard about it over at the Silver Queen this morning. Something about you suspecting he might have been involved in Thad Kelly's death?"

"I can't prove that. And even if he was, he still has to be laid to rest."

"That's true. It's a mighty decent thing for you to do, Mr. Fargo."

Fargo shook his head. He didn't want any credit for his actions. That was just the sort of man he was.

The hour was past midday now, and the work he had done so far had left Fargo with a thirst. He headed for the Silver Queen in search of a cool beer.

Sawtell, the proprietor of the place, stood at the end of the bar. He greeted Fargo, then said, "I hear you brought in Duffy's body."

"That's right," Fargo confirmed with a nod.

"I'd wager a considerable amount that he's the one who bushwhacked you and shot Thad last night. He's caused trouble in here before, and that ambush is just the sort of thing he'd do. He was a bad loser."

"That thought crossed my mind," Fargo admitted. He didn't say anything about his other theory, that someone had killed Duffy in order to divert suspicion onto him.

"I guess that cave-in was a sort of rough justice, then," Sawtell went on. "Have a drink?"

"That's what I'm here for," Fargo said.

He lingered in the saloon for a while, talking to Sawtell as he quenched his thirst with a cool beer. Then he headed across the street toward the hotel. Victorio and Guillermo Soto weren't standing on the porch now.

They were still staying at the hotel, though, as Everett confirmed for Fargo. The Trailsman's presence still made the hotel keeper nervous. Let him stew, Fargo thought. It was good penance for the hard time the man had given Rosa McLeod.

Fargo jerked his head toward the stairs. "The Sotos up in their rooms?" he asked.

"Well, yes, but . . . I'm not sure they want to be disturbed."

Fargo said, "I don't give a damn what they want. Which rooms are they in?"

He could tell from Everett's expression that the man didn't want to answer, but Everett was afraid not to. After a second's hesitation, he said, "The old man is in Fourteen, the younger one in Fifteen."

Fargo grunted. He wasn't going to say thank you to a polecat like Everett. He turned away from the desk and went up the stairs, taking them two at a time.

Guillermo looked surprised to see Fargo standing there when he opened his door in response to the Trailsman's sharp knock. "What are you doing here, gringo?" he snapped.

"I could ask the same of you," Fargo said. "I thought you and your pa were going back to Santa Fe."

"We decided to rest our horses for a few days before we start home," Guillermo replied. "Not that it's any of your business what we do."

"You wouldn't be hanging around so you can cause more trouble for Jim and Rosa McLeod, are you?"

Guillermo sneered. "I want nothing more to do with that ungrateful slut. I offered her my affections, and she was a fool to turn them down."

Fargo wanted nothing more at that moment than to plant his fist in the middle of Guillermo's arrogant young face. But he had other things on his mind, too, so he suppressed the impulse and asked, "Where were you this morning?"

"What do you mean? I was here, of course. Where else would I be?"

"Out at a little silver mine southwest of town, maybe?" Fargo suggested as he casually hooked his thumbs in his gun belt. "A claim that belonged to a man named Duffy?"

Guillermo frowned at him and appeared to be genuinely puzzled as he shook his head. "I have no idea what you're talking about, gringo."

The door of room fourteen opened, and Victorio Soto's cracked old voice said, "Guillermo! What are you doing talking to this gringo?"

"He came here to pester me with ridiculous questions, Father," Guillermo answered.

"Say no more! Go back in your room. We agreed that these gringos and their affairs were no longer any business of ours."

"Sí," Guillermo said with a sullen glare. He shut the door in Fargo's face.

Soto stepped closer to gaze up at Fargo. Short and whip-thin, the old man reminded Fargo of a ferret. Soto's lips were drawn into thin lines as he said, "Leave us alone, gringo. We want nothing to do with you. If you do anything to harm my son, I will kill you myself!"

"Why would I want to harm your son?" Fargo drawled. "If he steers clear of me, I'll steer clear of him . . . unless I find out he had something to do with killing a friend of mine."

"Guillermo has killed no one! If you say different, then you are a liar!" The old man's defiant look challenged Fargo to do something about the insult.

Fargo just laughed coldly. "I'm not saying anything . . . yet." Let Soto make of that what he would. Fargo didn't mind a bit if they considered him a threat. That might prod them into doing something to reveal what they were up to.

Soto turned on his heel and went back into his room, closing the door with more force than was necessary. Fargo chuckled and shook his head. He had himself a couple of enemies in those two.

But he had known that already.

He still had a room in the hotel, the room where Rosa had stayed the night before. He went into it, stretched out on the bed, and took a nap. Like most frontiersmen, Fargo believed in sleeping whenever he had the chance, because a fella never knew when trouble might force him to stay awake and on his feet for days on end.

As he settled his head on the pillow, he caught a whiff of the faint scent from Rosa's hair. It stirred something within him, but he put those thoughts aside and dozed off.

When he woke up late that afternoon, he washed up with water from the basin on the dressing table and put on a clean shirt, then left the hotel and walked down the street to the office of the Drummond Mining Company. Lily was inside at the front desk, right where he expected to find her.

"Mr. Fargo!" she greeted him with a smile. "I was worried that you might have forgotten you said you'd have dinner with me tonight."

"I never forget a dinner engagement with a beautiful woman," Fargo told her.

Lily's eyes sparkled happily behind the spectacles. "What a nice thing to say. If you'll give me a few minutes, I'll be through here." She gestured at the paperwork spread out across the desk. "Then we can go down to the hotel for dinner."

"Sounds good to me," Fargo said. He picked up one of the ladder-back chairs, turned it around, and straddled it. As he rested his arms on the chair back, he watched Lily sorting papers and entering figures in a book.

After a few minutes, he became aware of a pink flush creeping across her fair-skinned features. As far as Fargo was concerned, it made her prettier than ever. After a few more minutes went by as she attempted to work, she finally took off her spectacles and looked at him.

"Mr. Fargo, you're staring at me," she accused.

"It's hard not to look at a beautiful woman," Fargo said.

"I'm certainly not beautiful. Most days I consider myself as plain as mud."

"Not hardly," Fargo said.

"Now, you take Miss McLeod. . . . *She's* beautiful."

"That she is," Fargo agreed, not mentioning the fact that he *hadn't* taken Rosa when he had the chance. "But there are all different kinds of beautiful, especially where women are concerned."

"You're just trying to flatter me. Don't think I don't appreciate it, Mr. Fargo, but it's not necessary."

"It's not flattery if it's true," Fargo said. "And why don't you call me Skye?"

"All right, I will . . . Skye." Lily closed the ledger book. "I think I'm done here. Let's go have dinner."

Fargo grinned as he got to his feet. "You won't get any argument from me, ma'am."

"Don't start that ma'am business," she said as she came out from behind the desk and offered him her arm. "You're Skye, and I'm Lily."

"Sounds fine to me," Fargo agreed.

Dinner in the hotel dining room was good, and the company was even better than the food. Fargo enjoyed talking to Lily. She was intelligent and more than willing to tell him about the life she had led back in Saint Louis.

"Henry was almost like a second father to me growing up, rather than a brother," she said. "There's almost twenty years' difference between our ages, you know." She smiled.

"When I came along, I was quite the surprise to my parents, as you might imagine."

"A pleasant surprise, I'd guess."

"I hope so. Then Henry went off to join the army and wound up in that war down in Mexico, and he was so dashing when he came home as an officer."

"Dashing" wasn't a word Fargo would have used to describe the rather stodgy Colonel Drummond, but he supposed Drummond might have appeared that way to a hero-worshipping younger sister.

"As soon as I got his letter telling me how he was coming out here to look for silver, I wrote right back suggesting that I join him," Lily went on. "But he insisted that I stay in Saint Louis to look after Mother, and of course he was right. Henry always is. After Mother passed on, though, there was nothing holding me there. Henry still tried to talk me out of it—he said life out here was too rough for me—but I wouldn't be dissuaded."

"In other words, you're stubborn," Fargo said.

Lily laughed. "As a mule. Sooner or later, I always get what I go after."

As she spoke, Fargo noted a new light shining in her eyes. He had been drawn to her from the first moment he saw her, and now he could tell that she felt the same way.

As if they were both aware of the subtle change that had taken place between them, they finished their dinner without any delay and didn't linger over their coffee. As Fargo escorted her upstairs to her room, she asked, "What are your plans for the evening, Skye?"

"I don't really have any," Fargo said. "After what happened last night, I'm not really in the mood for a poker game."

"Yes, I can understand why you wouldn't be. That was a terrible thing. . . . But I don't really want to talk about that tonight. I hope you don't think that makes me awful."

"Of course not." They came to a stop in front of the door to her room. "Here we are."

Lily turned toward him and rested a hand on his arm. "Skye, why don't you come in for a while?"

Fargo smiled faintly. "I don't reckon your brother would think that was proper," he said.

"As much as I love Henry, right now I don't really care what he would think," Lily said. "I'd like to spend more time with you, Skye."

"I'd like that, too," Fargo said.

She cocked her head a little to the side. "Then what's stopping us from getting to know each other better?"

"Not a thing I can think of," Fargo said.

6

Lily came into his arms as soon as she had lit the lamp and Fargo had closed the door behind them. Desire had grown strong in Fargo, and he could tell from the hungry way her lips found his that she felt the same way.

She put her arms around his neck and molded her body to his. Her lips parted eagerly as his tongue slid between them. Fargo felt the heated touch of her tongue against his as they swooped and circled in a sensuous dance.

He cupped the back of her neck with his left hand while his right roamed down her back to the swelling curve of her hips. His fingers plucked at the pins in her hair until it came loose and tumbled in honey-colored waves around her shoulders. At the same time, he pressed on her rump, urging her closer to him. His hardening shaft prodded against the soft warmth of her belly. Her hips moved, grinding her pelvis into him.

Lily pulled her head back, breaking the kiss as she gasped, "Let's get these clothes off, Skye!"

That was the best idea Fargo had heard in a long time.

He tossed his hat onto a chair. Lily turned so that he could unfasten the buttons running down the back of her dress. When he had them undone, he spread the dress over her shoulders and slid it down over her arms and hips. She wore a shift and a petticoat underneath it. She was slender enough that she had no need of a corset.

When she turned to face him, he saw the erect buds of

her nipples pressing against the thin fabric of the shift. That reminded him of how Rosa McLeod had looked when she was waiting for him in his room the night before. Rosa's breasts were larger; full, firm globes rather than the smaller, pear-shaped breasts of Lily Drummond.

But that was one of the good things about women as far as Skye Fargo was concerned. They were all attractive, no matter what shape or size they were.

He put his hands on Lily's shoulders and moved aside the thin straps holding up the shift. The garment dropped, bunching around her waist as it bared her breasts. Fargo's hands cupped them. His thumbs stroked the hard nipples, which were smaller and pinker than Rosa's.

Fargo told himself to stop making those comparisons. He was with Lily now, and that was what he wanted.

She closed her eyes in pleasure and tipped her head back a little as Fargo continued caressing her. He leaned forward, sucked one nipple between his lips and tongued it, then the other. Lily said, "Ah," and ran her fingers through his thick, dark hair.

Fargo hooked his fingers inside the shift and petticoat and pushed them down over her hips. They puddled on the floor around her feet. That left her nude except for her spectacles and a pair of stockings rolled just above her knees.

He ran his eyes over her, from the waves of fair hair to the pert breasts, to the smooth, milky belly, to the trim thighs with the triangle of slightly darker hair where they joined. It was beyond him how she could ever considered herself plain as mud. He thought she was breathtakingly lovely.

"Now it's your turn, Skye," she said as she stepped closer to him. She took hold of his buckskin shirt and peeled it up and over his head, revealing the broad, muscular chest matted with dark brown hair.

Fargo took off his gun belt and hung it over the back of the room's only chair. He unstrapped the sheathed Arkansas toothpick from his leg and placed it on the seat of the chair. That left his high-topped boots and the buckskin trousers.

"Let me help you with those boots," Lily offered. "Sit on the edge of the bed."

Fargo did, and Lily moved in front of him, with her back turned toward him. She bent over and grasped his right boot as he lifted that leg. From this angle, Fargo had an extremely enticing view of her rear end, with the slick, pink folds of her sex peeking out from between her thighs.

"I used to help Henry with his boots like this," Lily said, then laughed. "Well . . . not *exactly* like this."

That was a relief, Fargo thought.

A moment later, she had both boots off of him, and he was so aroused that his erect member was uncomfortably confined in his trousers. As he stood up, her fingers flew to the buttons of the trousers and deftly unfastened them. He sighed in relief when she pushed down the trousers and his underwear and the long, thick shaft sprang free.

"Oh, my God, Skye," Lily breathed as she wrapped both hands around his manhood. She backed toward the bed, holding on to him so that he had no choice but to go with her—not that he would have wanted to be anywhere else in the world at this moment.

Lily put her spectacles aside, then sat down and bent forward so that she could kiss the head of his shaft. Her tongue flickered out and licked hotly around the crown. That intimate caress made Fargo's manhood throb from base to tip. Still holding it with one hand, Lily opened her lips wide and took the head in her mouth. Her tongue swirled around it. Fargo groaned as the exquisite sensations she created cascaded through him.

After several moments of delicious torment as she

sucked and licked him, Fargo put his hands on her shoulders and moved her away from him. "Your turn," he said as he eased her down onto her back on the bed. Her thighs parted instinctively, giving him his best look yet at her femininity. She was so wet that tiny droplets of moisture beaded like dew on the fine-spun hair around her opening.

Fargo knelt between her legs and used his thumbs to spread the slick folds even more. He began kissing and licking her. Her hips bucked up from the bed as his tongue found the little bud that was the center of her pleasure. Lily gasped in delight.

Fargo knew that neither of them could stand to wait much longer for fulfillment, but he wanted to make this experience as good for Lily as he possibly could. His lips and tongue and fingers worked her higher and higher toward her peak as her head tossed from side to side and the cords stood out in her neck as she strained toward release.

After several minutes, a series of shudders ran deeply through her. Her thighs clamped around his head with surprising strength. He speared his tongue into her and made her hips pump even harder.

Then she sagged back onto the bed as every muscle in her body seemed to go limp at once. Her breasts heaved as she tried to catch her breath. Fargo gave her a moment to recover, but his own need was still strong and wouldn't be denied for long. He lifted himself and poised between her thighs as he brought the head of his shaft to her opening. Her eyes flew open as she felt it touch her.

Then she exclaimed, "Oh!" as Fargo's hips surged forward and he sheathed the entire length of his manhood inside her, filling her to the brim.

Fargo drove in and out of her. Her legs lifted and locked together above his pistoning hips. She wrapped her arms around his neck and pulled his face down to hers. Their mouths met again in an urgent kiss.

After only a dozen thrusts, Lily began to spasm again. Fargo felt his own culmination boiling up inside him, so he drove into her again and didn't try to hold back. His climax erupted from him, filling her as she bucked and groaned underneath him.

After cresting together, they clung to each other as they took the long, slow, lazy slide down the other side. When Fargo's member finally softened enough to slip out of her, he rolled to the side and took her with him, so that they wound up lying on their sides, with their arms still wrapped around each other.

"Skye, that . . . that was lovely," Lily whispered. "But no more, please. Not right now. I . . . I'm not sure I'll ever fully catch my breath again!"

"I reckon you will," Fargo told her. "You seem pretty resilient."

She laughed and reached down to wrap her fingers around his manhood. "We'll just see who's the most resilient, Mr. Fargo," she said with a smile. "I'll bet that I'm ready for more before—" She stopped short, her eyes widening in surprise as she felt him stir. "Skye, is that . . . I mean, you can't possibly be . . . How in the world can you . . ."

"Clean living," Fargo said with a grin.

Over the next few days, Fargo and Lily discovered just how resilient they both were. They were together every chance they could find, although Lily drew the line at neglecting her work in the office of her brother's mining company.

She didn't draw the line at much of anything else, though. They explored each other's body to the fullest. Lily proved to be an eager, inventive lover. Fargo enjoyed her company so much, he almost forgot about what had happened the night of his arrival in Las Vegas.

But only almost. He still wondered about the attempt on his life that had wound up with Thad Kelly dead, instead of him. Most people in the settlement seemed to think that the prospector, Duffy, had been the bushwhacker. Fargo wasn't totally convinced of that, however. For that reason, he was doubly careful when he walked along the street, especially at night. Death could lurk in any dark alley.

Victorio and Guillermo Soto were still in Las Vegas, too. Fargo was convinced that they were up to no good. Otherwise they would have started back to Santa Fe before now. They kept to themselves in their hotel rooms, though, and didn't act like they were looking for trouble.

Despite the potential for danger that Fargo sensed was still lurking here, the days and nights passed quietly, even enjoyably. Certainly the nights qualified. Fargo and Lily made love in every way that two people possibly could.

She was excited, but in a much different way, when he stopped by the mining company office one morning. "I expect Henry back with the ore wagons today," she told Fargo. "He keeps to a fairly strict schedule."

That didn't surprise Fargo. The colonel might not be in the army anymore, but he still approached life like an officer.

Fargo was glad to hear the news, too. If Drummond was bringing the ore wagons into town, that meant Jim McLeod would be coming along, too. Fargo was looking forward to seeing the old mountain man again and hearing about how he and Rosa were adjusting to life out at the Lily Belle Mine.

"Maybe I'll ride out to meet the wagons," Fargo suggested. "I don't reckon Jim would mind having an extra guard along for part of the way."

"Oh, I'm sure that's not necessary, Skye," Lily said. "Mr. McLeod struck me as being quite competent."

"He is," Fargo agreed, "but if those owlhoots jump the wagons again, it won't hurt to have another rifle along to fight them off."

"Well, that's true. Just be careful." She stood up from behind the desk, took her spectacles off, and came around to slip into his embrace. Just before he kissed her, she murmured, "Now that I've found you, I wouldn't want anything to happen to you."

"Me, neither," Fargo said with a smile. Then his lips were busy drinking in all the hot sweetness of Lily's lips.

It would have been easy to let her distract him, but he wanted to see McLeod again, and besides, Lily had work to do. She had explained to him how her brother depended on her to keep track of how many tons of ore the mine was producing and how much silver per ton assayed out of those rocks. She kept track of all the company's dealings with the federal government, too.

Lily told Fargo that if the wagons left the mine at first light, as was Drummond's habit, they would arrive in Las Vegas sometime that afternoon. Fargo ate lunch with her at the hotel, then headed down to the livery stable to get the Ovaro ready to ride. He figured on meeting the wagons somewhere out on the flats west of the settlement.

He was pulling the cinches tight on the stallion's saddle when the old man who ran the stable said, "I'm glad you didn't come by a mite earlier, Fargo. Them Mexes you had trouble with was here, and I don't need no ruckuses in my stable."

Fargo looked around at the old-timer with a frown. "You mean Victorio and Guillermo Soto?"

"I don't know their names. I just heard talk around town about how you tangled with 'em before at the hotel, you and that big hombre McLeod. Folks been speculatin' about how long it's gonna be before all hell breaks loose again."

The elderly stable keeper had been forking hay into the stall next to the one where Fargo's Ovaro was kept. He had stopped working now and leaned on his pitchfork instead. He was a skinny, leathery old man with a white wisp of a beard that hung down below his chin and one bad eye that had gone milky. Fargo didn't particularly like him, but as far as he could tell, the old man took good care of the horses stabled here, so that was all that really mattered.

Still, the man's tone irritated Fargo. "I'm not looking for trouble with the Sotos or anybody else," he snapped.

"Didn't say you were, son. Can't say the same for those greasers, though, 'specially the young one. He's just spoilin' for a fight."

Fargo couldn't argue with that. He felt the same way about Guillermo Soto.

"You say they were here before?"

"Yep, them and those four hombres who work for 'em."

"What did they want?"

"What do you reckon they wanted?" the old man asked in a crotchety voice. "They saddled up their hosses and rode out. Well, a couple o' the hired hands saddled up for the old man and the boy. Can't expect rich folks like that to get their own hands dirty throwin' a saddle on a hoss."

"They rode out and they haven't come back yet?" Maybe he was being overly suspicious, Fargo thought, but that didn't bode well.

"Ain't seen hide nor hair of 'em since they left."

"Maybe they finally started back to Santa Fe."

"Not unless they were plannin' on goin' a mighty long way around. They was headed west when they left town. I watched 'em."

West, Fargo thought . . . toward the foothills where Colonel Drummond's mine was located.

The mine where Rosa McLeod now lived and worked.

"I'm obliged," Fargo said with a curt nod. He swung up into the saddle and rode out of the livery stable.

The Ovaro was ready to run, so Fargo gave him his head. Las Vegas soon fell behind as horse and rider swept westward over the flats. Fargo wasn't sure what Guillermo Soto and his father were up to, but it couldn't be anything good. He didn't figure that only six men would attack those ore wagons, but anything was possible when you were dealing with hombres as proud and stiff-necked as those two.

Besides, Fargo suddenly thought, how did he know there was no connection between the Sotos and the gang of outlaws that had gone after Colonel Drummond's ore shipments in the past? That would be quite a coincidence, but stranger things had happened, he supposed.

After a mile or so, Fargo pulled the Ovaro back to a trot. The stallion had the most strength and stamina of any horse Fargo had ever seen, but it never hurt to conserve some of those things in case they were needed later. Even so, the pace Fargo set now still ate up the ground.

After a while, he spotted a thin column of dust rising several miles ahead, across the arid plain. That dust was probably coming from the ore wagons, Fargo thought. He hitched the Ovaro into a slightly faster gait.

A few moments later, he noticed that the dust had stopped moving and was now dissipating in the hot, turgid breeze that blew over the flats. That brought a frown to Fargo's face as he wondered why the wagons had halted.

The frown deepened as that same breeze suddenly brought the faint, distant popping of gunshots to Fargo's ears.

Not again, Fargo thought as he leaned forward in the saddle and jammed his bootheels into the Ovaro's flanks, sending the stallion leaping ahead in a gallop. Damn it, not again.

He was at least a mile from where the fight was taking place, maybe more. Sounds could travel a long way over this flat landscape. Fargo was glad now that he had held the Ovaro in and saved some of the big black-and-white horse's strength. The stallion stretched out, fairly flying over the brush-dotted sand and gravel.

As he always did when he found himself in a situation like this, Fargo hoped that the Ovaro wouldn't step in a hole. At this speed, that would be a disaster, leaving the stallion with a broken leg, at best. At worst, horse and rider might both break their necks.

The Ovaro's keen instincts avoided any such dangers, though, and in a few minutes Fargo came within sight of the wagons. He saw immediately why they had stopped. The lead mules in each team were down, probably shot from ambush. Fargo wasn't sure where the bushwhackers could have hidden, but they had managed somehow.

With the leaders killed, the wagons couldn't move. They were stuck right where they were. That meant the outlaws who were after the silver ore could pick off the men with the wagons at their leisure. As Fargo came closer, he spotted some puffs of powder smoke coming from a cluster of small boulders. That was where the varmints were hidden now, he thought, but that couldn't have been where they were when they ambushed the wagons. Jim McLeod would have checked out those rocks before leading the vehicles past them. Fargo was certain of that.

He tugged on the reins and sent the Ovaro circling wide to the right as he pulled the Henry from its saddle sheath. His goal was a small, rocky ridge that would give him some cover and an angle into that cluster of boulders.

Some of the outlaws must have noticed him. Smoke

jetted toward him, and slugs kicked up dirt and gravel a few yards to his left. He was just out of accurate rifle range, he thought with a tight, grim smile. But he couldn't reach that ridge without getting close enough to be in range of those outlaw guns.

He'd just have to chance it and trust to the Ovaro's speed, he told himself. The big horse flashed over the ground. The bullets came closer, but the Ovaro never slowed.

Fargo felt the hot gust of a slug as it whipped past his face. He couldn't hear the whine of the bullet over the thundering hoofbeats of the Ovaro. The ridge loomed ahead of him. Almost like a Pony Express rider about to change mounts, he slipped his feet out of the stirrups, swung his left leg over the stallion's back, and landed running, the Henry clutched tightly in one hand as he reached back with the other hand to slap the Ovaro's rump. His hat flew off his head as he let his momentum carry him forward in a dive that landed him behind the little wrinkle of rock and dirt that formed the ridge. He hit hard enough that the impact knocked the air out of his lungs for a few seconds.

Looking back over his shoulder as he caught his breath, Fargo saw that the Ovaro had whirled around and was racing away as fast as he could, getting out of rifle range again. That slap on the rump while Fargo was performing the running dismount had been the signal for the stallion to do that.

He worked the Henry's lever as he squinted his eyes against the little cloud of dust and grit the Ovaro's hooves had kicked up with the sharp turn. Bullets smacked into the front of the ridge but couldn't penetrate it.

Fargo snaked the rifle barrel over the crest and fired, cranking off three rounds as fast as he could jack the lever. He didn't have anything to aim at except those boulders, but he knew that if he got a few slugs bouncing around in there, they would create some havoc among the outlaws.

The bushwhackers sent a hail of bullets back at him, and from the number of shots, Fargo knew that at the very least, he had distracted them from their attack on the ore wagons. He ducked his head and kept it down as the outlaws vented their fury at him with a thunderous volley.

They couldn't keep it up forever. For one thing, Fargo heard renewed firing coming from the wagons and knew that Drummond, McLeod, and the other men were taking advantage of the distraction he had provided for them. Those slugs had to be ricocheting around in the boulders, too. When a lull came, Fargo opened fire again.

A moment later, a dozen men on horseback burst from the rocks and galloped off to the north. Once again, the outlaws were giving up on the fight because they had met more resistance than they expected.

Fargo sent a couple of bullets after them to hurry them on their way. He didn't abandon the cover of the ridge until the riders were well out of rifle range. The ridge wasn't very big, but it had been enough to help him accomplish his goal, which was to send the outlaws fleeing again.

He let out a shrill whistle as he got to his feet. The Ovaro galloped up while Fargo was retrieving his hat. He settled the Stetson on his head, then swung up into the saddle and headed for the wagons, anxious to find out whether the attack had done any damage other than killing half a dozen mules.

Colonel Drummond walked out to meet him as he approached. From the grim expression on the colonel's face, Fargo knew that something bad had happened. He felt a pang of worry for his old friend Jim McLeod.

Drummond had a rifle in one hand. He lifted the other

in greeting and said, "Mr. Fargo, you've shown up in the nick of time once again. Those scoundrels might have killed us all if your arrival hadn't tipped the odds against them."

"They still outnumbered us," Fargo pointed out as he dismounted. "They just didn't want to pay the price it would have taken to get their hands on that ore. Where's Jim?"

Drummond's expression grew even bleaker. "Under one of the wagons. He was hit, Fargo. It's bad."

Fargo had been afraid of that when McLeod hadn't come out to meet him along with Drummond. "Take me to him," he said.

As they walked toward the wagons, Fargo counted heads. The other two drivers appeared to be all right. Fargo saw that McLeod had doubled the number of guards to six, no doubt recruiting some of the men who worked as miners in the Lily Belle for the job. A couple of them were wounded, one using his rifle for a crutch as he stood beside a wagon, the other having another guard tie a rag around his bloodstained upper arm as a crude bandage.

That meant McLeod was the only one who was badly hurt.

The realization made suspicion stir again in Fargo's brain. Even though he hadn't seen any sombreros on the outlaws who had attacked the ore wagons, that didn't mean there was no connection between them and the Sotos. Maybe those weren't even the same gunmen who had jumped the wagons before. They could have been killers hired by Victorio Soto to get rid of Jim McLeod.

If that turned out to be the case, then where were Victorio and Guillermo?

At the mine, maybe, going after Rosa?

Fargo's jaw tightened. He wanted to get to the Lily

Belle and make sure Rosa was all right. But before he could do that, he had to see how badly her father was hurt.

He spotted the dark, bulky shape lying under the middle wagon. McLeod wasn't moving.

"What happened?" Fargo asked Drummond. "How did they manage to bushwhack you out here in the middle of all this open ground?"

"I'm still not sure," the colonel said with a shake of his head. "All I know is that a volley of shots rang out with no warning, and the leaders on all three teams went down. So did McLeod. Then those gunmen and their horses seemed to come out of the ground over there." He waved a hand toward the north. "They galloped over to those rocks and took cover, then started concentrating rifle fire on us." Drummond sighed. "I don't understand it. McLeod scouted the rocks and said they were clear. And the initial volley didn't come from there."

Fargo had an idea what had happened, but he could confirm his theory later. Right now, he wanted to see just how bad a shape McLeod was in.

He knelt beside the wagon and saw that the mountain man's barrel chest rose and fell in a ragged rhythm. McLeod's buckskin shirt was sodden with blood from at least three wounds through his body. His rugged face above the bushy beard was drained of color. Fargo heard a rattling wheeze as McLeod drew breath and knew that the big man's lungs were filling up with blood. McLeod didn't have long to live, mere minutes, more than likely.

"Jim," Fargo said. "Jim, can you hear me?"

McLeod's eyelids fluttered feebly. He forced his eyes open. His fingers dug into the dirt beside him.

"Skye . . . ? Is that . . . you?"

McLeod's voice was a husky whisper, a faint shadow of its usual booming tone. Fargo leaned closer and said,

"Yeah, it's me. I want you to listen to me, Jim. I'm going to take care of Rosa. I swear it. She'll be fine."

McLeod managed to smile, although the expression was half grimace, too. He rasped, "You knew what I . . . wanted to hear . . . as I was crossin' the divide . . . didn't you . . . Skye?"

Fargo gripped his friend's hand. "It's the truth. You don't have to worry about her. I'll see to that."

"I . . . I'm much obliged." McLeod coughed, and bright red blood dribbled from both corners of his mouth. He peered up at Fargo and said, "One more . . . thing . . ."

"What is it?"

"Get the . . . sons o' bitches . . . who done this to me!" McLeod's fingers clenched tight on Fargo's as he spoke.

The Trailsman returned the grip as he leaned closer and vowed, "Every damn one of them, Jim."

With that, a long sigh came from McLeod, and his hand went limp. Fargo lowered it to the ground. His friend was gone, but at least McLeod had died knowing that Rosa would be protected and his death would be avenged.

Now all Fargo had to do was make good on those promises. He intended to, even if those were the last things he ever did.

7

"I have reason to believe that Rosa McLeod may be in danger," Fargo told Colonel Drummond. "I'd like to go on to Las Vegas with you to make sure you get there safely, but I can't. I need to get to the mine."

"Of course," Drummond said with a nod. "We'll continue on the best we can, but it'll to be slow going. We'll have to unhitch those dead mules and make do with short-handed teams."

Fargo picked up the Ovaro's reins. "Tell me how to get to your mine."

"Certainly. Continue due west until you reach the foothills. You'll see how they form a saddle, just to the north. Go through there and you'll find a little valley running to the northwest. Follow it for a mile and you'll come to a cliff. The mine tunnel is at the base of that cliff. You'll be able to see the mouth of it, as well as the buildings, without any problem."

Fargo nodded. The place sounded easy enough to find. He swung up onto the stallion's back and said, "Keep your eyes open, Colonel. That bunch could double back and hit you again before you get to town."

"I know. But we'll fight our way through if we have to, just like my regiment did at Vera Cruz." Drummond sighed. "We'll load poor McLeod's body in one of the wagons and take it in with us, of course. God, I'm starting to wish I had taken that offer."

Fargo had started to pull the Ovaro's head around, but he paused to look back at the colonel. "What offer?"

"A month and a half ago, right after we started taking out ore with good color, a mining syndicate in Chicago offered to purchase the claim from me. Their offer was a lucrative one, but I felt like the mine had the potential to be even more valuable in the long run, so I turned it down. If I had accepted, getting the ore to Las Vegas would be the syndicate's problem now, not mine, and Jim McLeod would still be alive."

"You can't know that for sure," Fargo said, but he suspected that Drummond was right.

The news of that offer from the mining syndicate was mighty interesting, too. Fargo couldn't help but wonder if it had some connection to all the troubles Drummond had been having.

He'd have to hash that out at another time. Right now he had to keep the first promise he had made to McLeod and see to it that Rosa was safe. Everything else would have to come later.

With a wave, Fargo rode away from the wagons. He made a quick detour to the north and soon spotted a dark line zigzagging across the ground. As he approached, that line turned into a slash in the earth about four feet wide and maybe twice that deep. It ended at a place where the banks had crumbled, providing a gentle enough slope so that horses could climb out of it.

That was where the bushwhackers had hidden themselves, Fargo knew. Sometime in the dim past, the earth had cracked here. The twisting gash would be invisible from a hundred yards away. That was why Jim McLeod had never seen it until it was too late. The mountain man hadn't ranged quite far enough away from the wagons in his scouting.

Fargo's jaw tightened. McLeod had paid for that mistake with his life.

Fargo turned the Ovaro and sent him toward the distant foothills at a run. He held the stallion under a full-out gallop because he knew it would take a couple of hours to reach the mine, and not even the magnificent Ovaro could keep up such a pace for that long. In a race like this, stamina mattered more than sheer speed.

Every half hour, Fargo dismounted and walked the horse for five minutes. The Ovaro tossed his head as if he wanted to keep running. Fargo wasn't going to ride his old friend into the ground, though, no matter what the stallion wanted.

He could see the foothills, but covering the distance to them was maddeningly slow. They seemed to hover there in the dry air, almost close enough to reach out and touch but always just out of reach. Fargo was very familiar with that phenomenon, having experienced it many times during his wanderings through the West. He told himself to be patient and keep moving. He was actually getting there as fast as he possibly could.

But that might not be fast enough, he knew. If Rosa was in danger from the Sotos, they had probably reached the mine already. They might have even timed their arrival to coincide with the attack on the ore wagons, if those two events were connected. Impatience gnawed at Fargo, and it took all his iron self-control to ignore it.

Finally, he could look at the foothills with the mountains looming behind them and tell that they were closer, and from that point on, the journey seemed to go faster. He entered the hills, saw the saddle Drummond had mentioned, and rode through the gap between ridges into the valley beyond.

It didn't take him long to find the Lily Belle Mine.

The dark mouth of the tunnel was easy to spot against the granite wall of the cliff. Four log buildings and several storage sheds constructed of timber hauled down from the hills were scattered near the tunnel opening. A small cabin was probably where Drummond lived when he was out here. Not far away were a bunkhouse for the miners and an adjacent cook shack. A hundred yards away stood a small, squat building with no windows. That would be where they kept the blasting powder, Fargo thought. Off to the other side was a corral with a few horses in it.

Fargo didn't see anyone moving around, didn't hear any work going on. Those weren't good signs. As he rode toward the buildings, the blast of a gun suddenly shattered the still air. Fargo reined in as he heard the bullet whine over his head. Whoever had fired the shot had aimed high, obviously intending for it to be a warning.

"Hello, the camp!" Fargo shouted as he lifted both hands and held them in plain sight. "Hold your fire! I'm friendly!"

A man holding a rifle stepped out of the open bunkhouse door. He had a bloody bandage tied around his head. He trained the rifle on Fargo and called, "Who the hell are you, mister?"

Fargo didn't like having guns pointed at him. It rubbed him the wrong way, and his instinct was to fight back.

But right now, he needed information, and he had a hunch the hombre with the rifle was one of Colonel Drummond's men, not an enemy.

"My name is Skye Fargo!" he said. "I'm looking for Rosa McLeod! Is she here?"

"You know damned good and well she's not!" the man shouted back.

Fargo's heart fell at the words. He heeled the Ovaro into motion again and sent the horse forward.

"Hold it!" the man with the rifle yelled. "Don't come any closer, damn it!"

Fargo ignored the warning. He kept his hands in sight, not giving the man any excuse to shoot him, but he didn't rein in until he reached the bunkhouse.

"I was a friend of Jim McLeod's," Fargo said. "What happened to his daughter?"

"'Was'?" the man repeated. "What in blazes do you mean by that?"

"The ore wagons were ambushed again on their way to Las Vegas," Fargo explained. "I came along and helped fight off the bushwhackers, but it was too late to help McLeod. He was gunned down during the fighting." Fargo shook his head. "He didn't make it, but before he died, I promised him I'd see that Rosa was all right."

The man finally lowered the rifle as a grim, humorless laugh came from him. "Well, you're too late for that, too, mister. She's gone. A bunch of Mexicans carried her off earlier this afternoon, after they shot the hell out of the place."

That was exactly the news Fargo had hoped he wouldn't hear when he reached the mine. His hunch had been right, but this was one time he would have been happier to be wrong.

Another man limped out of the bunkhouse. He had a bloodstained bandage wrapped around his thigh. "Take it easy, Danvers," he told the first man. "I've heard of this fella Fargo. He's the one they call the Trailsman. He's friends with the boss and Miss Lily." The man limped forward and held up a hand to Fargo. "Name's Hutch."

Fargo shook with the man, then said, "All right if I get down?" He was anxious to get on the trail of whoever had kidnapped Rosa, but first he had to find out exactly what had happened.

"Sure," Hutch nodded. "Danvers, get the other fellas out here."

Four men emerged from the bunkhouse with Danvers a

moment later, bringing with them rifles and grim faces. Fargo nodded to them, then asked Hutch, who seemed to be the spokesman, "What happened?"

"You know the colonel started to Las Vegas this morning with three loads of ore. McLeod suggested that he ought to take half the crew with him as guards. The rest of us stayed here to keep working the mine, although we couldn't do as much as usual because we were gonna be shorthanded for a couple of days."

Fargo nodded his understanding and said, "Go on."

"Miss Rosa stayed behind, too, to cook for us. She's been a real godsend, Mr. Fargo. None of the rest of us can rustle vittles worth a damn."

Fargo restrained his impatience and nodded again.

"Most of us were in the mine a couple of hours ago when those bastards showed up," Hutch went on. "They headed straight for the boss's cabin. Miss Rosa's been stayin' there with her pa, while the colonel's been bunkin' with us. Danvers and I happened to be fetching some tools from one of the sheds when we saw them come riding in, and we knew right away they were up to no good. We ran for the tunnel to warn the other boys, and they started shooting at us." He touched his wounded leg. "That's how I got this crease. It knocked me down, and Danvers had to haul me the rest of the way."

Danvers grunted. "Hell, you'd have done the same thing for me, Hutch."

"More than likely. Anyway, we made it to the tunnel, where our guns were, and we tried to fight our way out and get to the colonel's cabin. We figured they had to be after Miss Rosa. They had us pretty well pinned down inside the tunnel, though. Danvers and a couple of the other men got hit when we tried to make it out. Then one of the Mexicans came out of the cabin, dragging Miss Rosa with him. . . ." Hutch shook his head. "She put up a hell of a fight, but it wasn't enough. Neither was anything we did. They carried her off."

"You didn't go after them?" Fargo asked. "You have horses."

"No offense, Mr. Fargo, but we're miners, not gun-fighters. And we had wounded men, too." Hutch shrugged. "I'm sorry. Maybe we should have tried to trail them. But we didn't."

Fargo told himself not to be too hard on the men. As Hutch had pointed out, Drummond had hired them to dig silver ore from the earth, not to fight off tough, well-armed raiders.

"Which way did they go?"

"South. Headed for Mexico, I guess."

Fargo knew better. Their destination was Santa Fe. But he supposed it wouldn't hurt anything to confirm that.

"Did you get a good look at the men? Can you describe them?"

"Well, there were six of them, I think. An old man, a youngster, and four in between. The old man and the boy were dressed fancier than the others. It was the boy who dragged Miss Rosa out of the cabin, while the old man and the others poured lead into the tunnel at us."

There was no doubt now, Fargo thought. All the talk by Victorio and Guillermo Soto about leaving Rosa alone and going back to Santa Fe had been just that—talk. Empty words. Fargo suspected that they had planned all along to take her with them by force if they had to.

"You said McLeod was killed when the ore wagons were attacked?" Hutch asked.

"That's right," Fargo said.

"That's a damned shame. I liked that old mountain man."

"So did I. That's why, before he died, I gave him my word that I'd protect Rosa."

"You're going after them?"

Fargo nodded.

"You'll be outnumbered six to one," Hutch pointed out.

"I've faced worse odds. I'll just have to whittle them down a mite."

"What about the colonel? Was he hurt?"

Fargo shook his head. "He and the other men were all right when I left them. Of course, they were still a ways outside of Las Vegas. The men who ambushed them could have doubled back."

"What do you reckon we ought to do?"

"Stay here and take care of the mine, as well as your wounded," Fargo said. "Drummond ought to be back sometime tomorrow afternoon, if he's all right."

"If you're goin' after those bastards who shot us up and took Miss Rosa, some of the boys might want to come with you."

Fargo shook his head. "No offense, Hutch, but I'm going to be traveling pretty fast."

"You really *don't* care about the odds, do you?"

A savage smile tugged at the corners of Fargo's mouth. "Like I said, I plan to whittle 'em down."

Fargo had no trouble picking up the trail left by the six riders as they headed south. They didn't seem to be trying to conceal their tracks, probably because their natural arrogance led them to believe that they didn't have to worry about any pursuit.

They would soon find out how wrong they were about that, Fargo told himself. To his experienced eyes, the signs they had left behind were as obvious as the mesas and rock spires that jutted up here and there in the mostly flat landscape.

The problem was that the afternoon was already fairly well advanced. Even though Fargo planned to push along at as fast a pace as the Ovaro could stand, he figured it was unlikely he would catch up to the Sotos before nightfall. That meant Rosa would have to spend at least one night on the trail with her captors before he even had a chance to rescue her.

Fargo hoped that he could count on the old man's sense of honor to keep Rosa safe, at least for the time being, but the attack on the mine today showed that Soto's honor sometimes lost out to what his son wanted, as well as to his own desire for revenge on the McLeod family.

If Guillermo laid a hand on her, Fargo would see to it that the young man paid for his crime—with his life, if necessary.

The terrain became even bleaker and more arid south of the mountains. If the men he was following kept going in that direction, they would soon cross over into California and reach the Mojave Desert, one of the most inhospitable places west of the Mississippi. For that reason, Fargo expected them to veer eastward, toward the Colorado River. Once they crossed the river, they could work their way southeast through Arizona until they reached one of the trails that would lead them back to New Mexico Territory.

That trip would take them several weeks. Fargo didn't intend to leave Rosa in their hands for anywhere near that long.

It was a race against the sun, one that Fargo inevitably lost. Even as the trail angled eastward, as he expected, the sun dipped below the western horizon. Night fell quickly out here in this semidesert country. Once the sun was gone, darkness descended like the dropping of a curtain. Millions of stars popped into view in the sky as it rapidly deepened from purple to blue to black, but they didn't cast enough light for Fargo to continue following the tracks left by his quarry.

Reluctantly, he called a halt for the time being, although he hoped that the moon might be bright enough later for him to resume following the tracks. In the meantime, both he and the Ovaro would get some much-needed rest.

Because he hadn't intended to spend the night out on the trail when he left Las Vegas, he hadn't brought many supplies with him. But he always had some jerky in his saddlebags, and he never went anywhere without a full canteen. After unsaddling the Ovaro, he poured a little water in his hat for the stallion, and as the horse drank, Fargo said, "There's a little bit of grass out here, big fella, so I reckon you won't starve. Neither will I, but we'll both be on short rations for a while. If it takes us a few days to catch up to those bastards, our bellies may get real well-acquainted with our backbones."

While the Ovaro grazed on some clumps of short, hardy grass, Fargo gnawed a strip of jerky, washed it down with a couple of sips of water, and then stretched out to get some rest. He knew the big stallion would warn him if any varmints, human or otherwise, came anywhere close. And even if he dozed off, Fargo knew that his own senses would remain partially alert. He had the knack of being able to come fully awake in the blink of an eye if he had to.

Fargo gazed up at the seemingly endless stars for a moment and wondered how Rosa was doing tonight. He sent up a quick prayer to *El Señor Dios* that those bastards who had carried her off hadn't harmed her.

For the next few hours, Fargo catnapped. The silvery light of the moon woke him as it rose. It was about three-quarters full tonight, so it gave off quite a bit of illumination. Following tracks by moonlight was a tricky business—you always ran the risk of losing the trail and wasting more time than you gained—but Fargo had done it before and his instincts told him he could do it again tonight. He'd just have to take it a little slower.

But even so, he ought to gain on the men he was following, he thought. He doubted if the Sotos would push on through the night. For one thing, as tough as that old man was, he would still need some rest.

As Fargo picked up the Ovaro's saddle, he said, "You ready to get moving again?" The stallion tossed his head, as if replying eagerly in the affirmative.

Fargo got the horse saddled up and then started following the tracks again, at a walk this time. For the moment, he could see them plainly enough so that he had no trouble staying on the trail. If that changed later on, he would decide what to do then.

The route followed by the Sotos still trended eastward, toward the Colorado River. There were some twists and turns along the way, because while the landscape might appear flat for the most part, it was really more rugged than it looked, and sometimes riders had to detour around natural obstacles.

About a hundred miles northeast of here, the river ran through the deepest, widest canyon Fargo had ever seen. There was nothing else like it anywhere on the frontier, at least not that Fargo knew of, and he had been just about everywhere from the Mississippi to the Pacific, from the Rio Grande to the Canadian border, and in a few cases, beyond. However, the Sotos had no reason to go in that direction, so he didn't expect to be seeing the big canyon on this trip.

Under other circumstances, rocking along in the saddle like this might have lulled him into a half sleep, but not tonight. Fargo was fully alert. He didn't want to ride into the enemy camp without being aware of it and find himself surrounded with no warning. Instead, his eyes were always on the move, roving from the tracks left behind by his quarry to the vast, stygian darkness up ahead.

After several hours, he caught a glimpse of light in the distance. It was just a tiny orange wink, but that was enough. Somewhere up there, a piece of wood in a campfire that had burned down mostly to embers had blazed up for a second, and Fargo's hawklike vision had spotted the glow.

His mouth quirked. Victorio and Guillermo Soto had lived too long in Santa Fe, surrounded by servants. They had forgotten—if indeed Guillermo had ever really known—that there were dangers out here. Most of the Ute Indians who roamed through this region hated white men, and the Apaches had been known to raid this far north from time to time. A man who built a campfire out here and left it burning all night was just asking for trouble.

Fargo hoped that the fire hadn't drawn the attention of any wandering war parties. He had enough on his plate to deal with already, what with rescuing Rosa from the Sotos.

Even though he couldn't see the fire anymore, he had its location fixed in his mind, and his instincts guided him straight toward it. After a while, he dismounted and went ahead on foot, leading the Ovaro. The night breezes were shifting around, so he stopped when he figured he was getting close enough to risk the other horses catching the Ovaro's scent. That might stir them up and alert the camp to the fact that something was going on.

With a pat on the shoulder for the stallion, Fargo whispered, "Stay here, big fella." Then he started forward again, staying low and using the few clumps of greasewood and rocks for cover. The moon had risen late, so he couldn't wait until it set. That wouldn't be until after sunrise. Like it or not, he would have to risk moving in on the camp while the silvery glow still washed over the landscape.

He dropped into a crouch, then onto hands and knees as he approached a small cluster of trees along the edge of a tiny stream. It was a good place to camp, except for the fact that the Utes probably stopped here to water their horses fairly often. Again, that was something Soto and Guillermo wouldn't know—but Fargo did.

About fifty yards away, he stretched out on his belly and studied the camp. Everything seemed quiet and peaceful. He spotted the dark shapes of the horses under the trees. One man stood guard, walking slowly around the camp with a rifle cradled in his arms. Fargo could hear the faint crunch of sand under his boots. Everyone else was asleep in bedrolls that were scattered around the remains of the fire.

Fargo was sure the guard was one of the vaqueros. He was confident he could crawl in and out of the camp without attracting the man's attention, but unfortunately, the same didn't hold true for Rosa. Fargo had a hunch she was tied up, and he didn't think he would be able to free her and get her out of the camp without the others realizing what was going on.

What he needed, he thought, was a distraction, and a smile curved his lips in the darkness as he began to figure out what he was going to do.

8

A rocky knoll rose on the far side of the creek, about twenty yards from the camp. Fargo backtracked until he was well away from the stream, then came to his feet and moved at a crouching run that paralleled the creek. When he judged that he had gone far enough, he turned and forded the creek, being careful not to splash too loudly in the water. Then he began circling toward that knoll opposite the camp.

Along the way, he picked up a few branches that had broken off the scrubby mesquite bushes dotting the landscape and plucked some dry grass. By the time he reached the knoll, he had an armload. He put it on the ground and knelt beside it, then used his knife to cut several pieces of fringe off his shirt.

In a matter of minutes, he had used the fringe to lash the branches together into a shape that roughly resembled that of a man. He took off his shirt, draped it over the stick figure, and then placed his hat on top of the makeshift scarecrow.

In good light, the thing wouldn't fool anybody for a second. But in the moonlight, it would cast a shadow like a man, and that was all Fargo needed it to do.

He carried the scarecrow to the top of the knoll and wedged the base of it between several rocks so that it stood upright. Then he piled most of the dry grass around it and twisted the remainder into a fuse about five feet long. The fuse led up the slope into the pile of grass.

Fargo hunkered next to the end of the fuse and tilted his head back to let out the yipping call of a coyote. It sounded like the real thing, but Indians used signals like that as they were closing in on an enemy's camp, and the Sotos and their men might know that. Fargo wanted to make them nervous.

Cupping his other hand around a lucifer to shield the flame, he snapped the match to life and held it to the end of the fuse. The strands of dry grass caught easily. Fargo waited just long enough to judge how fast it was burning, then stood up and sprinted away from the creek, taking the same roundabout path he had followed to get there.

He heard voices across the creek and knew that the coyote cry had roused the men from their sleep. Right about now, they would be looking around, wondering if that had been a real coyote or if they were in danger of being attacked by Utes or Apaches. He hurried back across the creek, staying as low as he could while he ran. Moments later, he dropped to hands and knees again and crawled toward the camp.

They had stirred the fire up and gotten it burning again, he saw. By the light of the flames, he watched as Soto, Guillermo, and the four vaqueros milled around, each of them holding a rifle. They were definitely on edge.

Most important, as far as Fargo was concerned, none of them was paying any attention to Rosa, who had sat up to see what was going on. Her bedroll was the closest to the creek, which was a lucky break for him. Since the men were all looking toward the knoll, which loomed dark and ominous, Fargo was able to crawl all the way to the edge of the circle of light cast by the fire.

He glanced toward the top of the knoll. The fuse ought

to be reaching the pile of dry grass anytime now, he thought. If it had gone out, he was going to find himself in a bad position in another minute or two when Rosa's captors turned around again.

Suddenly, with no warning, the dry grass blazed up. A couple of Soto's men cried out in fear as the orange glare of the flames filled the sky above the knoll. Silhouetted against that glare was the scarecrow Fargo had made. The flickering light cast its ominous shadow down the slope, stretching it so that it almost reached the creek.

All six men whipped their rifles to their shoulders and started firing. The shots rolled out like thunder as they sent a storm of lead at the bizarre shape on top of the knoll.

While that was going on, Fargo surged to his feet and dashed to Rosa's side. The Sotos and their men never heard him over the roar of gunshots. Fargo dropped to his knees beside Rosa. The Arkansas toothpick was already in his right hand. His left went around her and clamped over her mouth to keep her from crying out in surprise. As she twisted in his grip, not knowing who he was, he put his mouth next to her ear and told her, "Rosa, it's me, Skye Fargo!"

She stopped fighting him and thrust her arms toward him. He saw the rope tied around her wrists. Carefully, so he wouldn't cut her, he slipped the tip of the blade under the ropes and started sawing. The knife was razor-sharp, so it took only a few seconds to cut through her bonds.

To his relief, Fargo saw that although Rosa's ankles were tied together, too, the rope had about a foot of slack in it. He grabbed it, looped it over the knife, and cut through it with one swift jerk. Then he stood up and pulled Rosa to her feet with him. He motioned for her to run.

Even though it seemed longer, less than a minute had gone by since Soto, Guillermo, and the vaqueros started shooting at the fire-lit scarecrow on top of the knoll. The stick figure was starting to fall apart. It wouldn't be long before the men realized that it didn't represent any threat. They had just been spooked and let their imaginations run wild.

Fargo backed away, resting his hand on the butt of his Colt as he did so. He could have drawn the revolver and gunned down several of the men from behind. But then he would have to deal with the others, and if he got himself killed, Rosa would still be in a bad fix, even if she managed to get away from the Sotos. Fargo wasn't sure she could survive out here in the middle of nowhere on her own.

For that reason, he retreated swiftly, turning and breaking into a run. So far, they had no idea what he had done, but that luck couldn't hold for much longer.

Sure enough, only seconds later Victorio Soto began shouting in Spanish for his men to hold their fire. Fargo figured that the old man had realized what was going on. He ran harder as he saw Rosa hurrying along in the moonlight ahead of him.

Fargo let out a shrill whistle as he lunged ahead and grabbed Rosa's arm. Behind them, Guillermo cried, "Rosa! She's gone! Get after her, you fools! *Andalé!*"

Hoofbeats pounded in the night air. The dark shape of the Ovaro loomed up, summoned by Fargo's whistle. Fargo and Rosa ran up to the stallion. Fargo leaped into the saddle, then reached down to grasp Rosa's arms as she lifted them to him. He swung her onto the horse's back behind him and told her, "Hang on tight!"

She wrapped her arms around his waist. He drove his bootheels into the Ovaro's flanks and sent the big stallion leaping forward in a gallop. Behind them, a shot rang out. Then Guillermo screamed, "No shooting! No shooting! You might hit Rosa!"

Fargo had been counting on that to give them a little extra time. The Ovaro stretched out, racing across the arid, moon-washed landscape. Faintly, he heard Soto ordering the men to saddle their horses.

A grin stretched across Fargo's face. They weren't going to catch the Ovaro. It would take several minutes for them to get their horses ready to ride, and by that time the stallion would have a good lead.

They might be safe for the moment, but they weren't out of the woods yet—not that there were any woods out here, except in the mountains, miles away. Fargo was sure that the Sotos would come after them and try to catch them before they got back to Las Vegas. He would have to try to give them the slip.

And once he had gotten Rosa safely back to the settlement, he would go looking for Soto and Guillermo again. He wanted to find out if they had had anything to do with Jim McLeod's death—and if they had, he intended to see that they faced justice for it.

It would be best if he and Rosa could find someplace to hole up for the rest of the night and let the pursuit go past them. Then they could circle around and give Soto and Guillermo the slip for good. Problem was, there weren't many places to hide out here. The terrain was too wide-open. The hills were too far away to the west.

So Fargo did what might have seemed odd to most people. He swung the Ovaro to the east and headed for the Colorado River.

This would be the long way around, but he thought it might be the safest. The Sotos would probably expect him to head straight back to Las Vegas. They wouldn't look for him in the opposite direction.

Rosa leaned forward, close enough for her hair to brush his ear as she said, "Skye, somehow I knew you would come for me. Are you taking me to my father?"

She couldn't see the grim line that his mouth became for a second at that question. Keeping what he felt out of his voice, Fargo said, "Not right now. We're going to concentrate on throwing them off our trail. Did they hurt you, Rosa?"

"Only my pride," she said. "Guillermo told me that my honor was in no danger, that he was taking me back to Santa Fe so that he could marry me in the church. He said that I would learn to love him, and that I would be happy. Ha! There was no chance of that, even before they kidnapped me!"

Fargo kept the Ovaro running flat-out for several more minutes. Then he slowed the stallion to a walk and then to a stop. Sitting there in the saddle with Rosa's arms clasped around him from behind, Fargo listened intently. He heard horses, but they sounded like they were far off in the distance to the west. His trick of turning toward the Colorado seemed to be working.

Of course, come morning those vaqueros would probably be able to pick up his trail again. Fargo hoped to have such a big lead on them by then that they could never catch him and Rosa.

The warmth of her body against his bare skin reminded him that he was stripped to the waist. He had left his shirt and hat back there on that blazing scarecrow. He had another shirt in his saddlebags, and he could buy a hat in Las Vegas, more than likely. But at the moment, he felt the soft heat of Rosa's full breasts pressed against his back as she hung on to him.

Fargo took a deep breath. The poor girl was an orphan now, as of this afternoon, and he had no business reacting like he was to her touch.

Knowing that in his heart and mind, though, and convincing his manhood of it were two different matters.

"Let's go," he said curtly. "I want to find a place to spend the rest of the night where they can't find us."

"That sounds like a good idea," Rosa said as Fargo heeled the stallion into a walk again. "It will be just fine with me if I never see Guillermo Soto and that wicked father of his again."

That wasn't true where he was concerned, Fargo mused. He planned on seeing both of the Sotos again. In fact, he was looking forward to it.

Because he wanted to be looking right at them when he asked them if they'd had anything to do with the death of Jim McLeod.

Judging by the moon and stars, it was well after midnight when Fargo and Rosa came to the great gorge of the river. This canyon was nothing to compare with the one farther northeast, but it was still deep and wide. The walls were broken and rugged, but Fargo knew there were trails leading down to the river. He searched until he found one. It was fairly steep, but he let the Ovaro pick his way down, trusting to the stallion's balance and instinct.

When they reached the bottom, Fargo heard the swift current of the river rushing along. Not much moonlight penetrated down here, so it was very dark. Fargo lit a match so they could see where they were going. They didn't want to take a tumble into the river.

The fast-moving stream ran between ledges on either side that were about forty feet wide. Large boulders and slabs of rock clustered along the base of the canyon wall, where they had fallen over an untold number of centuries. The bottom of this gorge wasn't exactly the safest place to be, but Fargo figured it would do for the night. It was better than wandering around up on the plains.

They came to a place where the boulders formed a ring around a good-sized open space. "It won't be all that comfortable," Fargo told Rosa, "but I reckon this is as good a place to camp as we're liable to find down here."

"Anyplace is fine, as long as it's away from those two devils. I don't think any man ever hated another as much as Victorio Soto hates my father."

Fargo dismounted and reached up to help her down. Holding the Ovaro's reins in one hand and Rosa's hand in the other, Fargo led them into the ring of stones. The ground in the clearing was rock with a thin layer of sand over it, which was better than bare rock, he supposed.

The air had a chill in it. Even in the summer, it cooled off quickly in this desert country once the sun was down. The air was too dry to retain any heat. Fargo rummaged around in his saddlebags until he found his extra buckskin shirt. He slipped it over his head.

"A shame," Rosa murmured as she put a hand on his arm. "I liked you the other way, with no shirt, Skye."

This was the worst possible time for her to be flirting with him, Fargo thought. He would have to discourage it, as gently as possible, of course. And he had to tell her what had happened to Jim. He didn't have any right to withhold that terrible news from her.

"There's no wood around to build a fire," he said. "I reckon we'll have to make do with a cold camp."

"That's all right. I'm sure we'll be able to stay warm."

Fargo didn't say anything in response to what was obviously a deliberately provocative comment. He unstrapped his bedroll from the saddle, then took the saddle itself off the stallion. Working in the dark didn't present a problem. Fargo had performed these tasks so many times they were like breathing to him. He didn't even have to think about them.

"Are you hungry?" he asked Rosa. "I have a little jerky."

"They fed me," she said. "Just tortillas and frijoles, but I'm all right. You go ahead."

Fargo sat down on one of the rocks and gnawed a piece of jerky. While he did that, Rosa took it upon herself to spread out the blankets. She arranged them so that they would have to roll up in them together, Fargo noted.

Of course, as chilly as the night was, that wasn't a bad idea.

Rosa sat down on the blankets and asked, "Were any of the men at the mine hurt? I know they were trying to fight off the Sotos, but they were pinned down inside the tunnel."

"A couple of them got winged, but they didn't seem to be hurt bad," Fargo said.

"Good. They've treated me well. Colonel Drummond is a gentleman, and he insists that the men who work for him act like gentlemen, too. I'm sorry some of them were hurt because of me."

"They'll be fine," Fargo assured her.

"Do you know whether the colonel got the ore wagons safely to Las Vegas? He was worried that they would be attacked again, but Papa promised him that they would make it through."

Fargo hesitated. He would rather face a pack of howling Comanches than have to tell Rosa what had happened. But she had a right to the truth.

Before he could answer, she patted the blankets beside her and said, "Come down here. I'm getting really cold, Skye."

He supposed that was true. She wore only a short-sleeved dress. Fargo moved to the blankets, and when Rosa leaned against him and rested her head on his shoulder, his arm instinctively went around her shoulders.

"I'm afraid I have bad news," Fargo began. "Outlaws

jumped the ore wagons on the flats west of Las Vegas, just like they did last time."

Rosa lifted her head, turning it so that she could look up at him. "Oh, no! Then the colonel was right to be worried. Did they steal the ore?"

Fargo thought it was a little odd that she didn't ask about her father first. Then he realized that she wasn't even going to allow herself to consider the possibility that he might have been hurt. If she didn't think about it, it couldn't happen. Fargo knew that wasn't true, but that didn't stop people from feeling that way sometimes.

"I happened to come along right after the outlaws made their move," he said. "Together, we were able to run them off. They never got their hands on the ore."

"Well, that's a relief. I'm sure my father was glad to see you."

"About that . . ." Fargo began.

"Skye," Rosa said sharply, "I'm warning you. I don't want to hear any bad news."

"And I don't want to tell you," Fargo said, "but I don't have any choice. Jim was wounded during the fighting."

Rosa sat up and turned toward him. Her hand found his and clutched it tightly.

"How bad?" she asked.

"Real bad. He lived long enough for me to talk a little to him, Rosa, but . . . he's gone."

A cry like that of a wounded animal came from her. She jerked her hand out of Fargo's and exclaimed, "No! It can't be true!" Her hands balled into fists, and she began pummeling his chest in anger and grief. "It's a lie. It's a lie!"

Fargo didn't try to stop her. She wasn't hurting him, and he knew the reaction wouldn't go on forever. After a moment, she stopped hitting him and sagged against him instead, wailing, "No, no, no!"

He put his arms around her and held her as she began to shake with sobs. Time passed, and he didn't know or care how long. He kept Rosa cradled against him and let nature take its course. She cried and cursed and cried some more. Finally, her sobs died away to sniffles, and she fell into a stupor that was half exhausted sleep and half shock.

They sat there together like that as the stars wheeled through the slice of ebony sky that was visible at the top of the gorge. Fargo dozed, and when he came fully awake, he saw that the sky was starting to turn gray with the approach of dawn.

Rosa sat beside him, wiping tears away from her eyes. She was still grief-stricken but composed as she said, "Tell me about it."

"I don't know that I ought to—"

"Tell me, Skye," she repeated. "It's important that I know . . . everything."

Fargo nodded. "All right. I reckon you've got more of a right than anybody else to hear it. Just know that I'd give anything not to have to tell you this."

"I know," she said. "And I would give anything not to have to hear it."

"Like I said, the outlaws jumped the ore wagons on the flats. There were about a dozen of them. They were able to hide in a gully that Jim didn't notice and kill the leaders in the mule teams so that the wagons couldn't go anywhere. Then they forted up in some rocks and started trying to pick off the men who were with the wagons."

"Was that when my father was hit?"

"No, they got him in the first volley, along with the mules. Like they were trying especially hard to make sure he was hit."

Rosa frowned. The sky was light enough now that

Fargo could make out the expression. "Because he was in charge of the guards?" she asked.

"Maybe."

"Why else would they have targeted him like that?"

Fargo answered that question with one of his own. "Did you hear Guillermo or his father say anything about an ambush while you were with them?"

Rosa stared at him, her mouth open in shock. "You think . . . *Dios mio!* . . . You think they planned the attack?"

"I don't know. I don't have any proof of that. But the possibility occurred to me. They raided the mine about the same time those other hombres ambushed the wagons. Those two things might be connected, or they might not be."

"That would explain so much," Rosa murmured as she looked down at the ground. Then she raised her eyes to Fargo again and went on. "But honestly, Skye, I never heard either of them say a word about such a thing. None of their vaqueros mentioned it, either."

"That doesn't clear them," Fargo pointed out. "It just means that we still have to find out the truth."

"And we will," Rosa said with grim, steely determination in her voice. "I can forgive them for what they did to me, but if they had anything to do with my father's death, I will kill them myself."

"You won't have to. I'll take care of that. That's one of the things I promised Jim, before he crossed the divide."

"What other promises did you make him?"

Fargo smiled. "That I would look after you."

She leaned over and wrapped her arms around his neck as she rested her tear-streaked face on his shoulder. "You have," she whispered. "You saved my life, Skye, because, I swear, if I had been doomed to spend the rest of my years with Guillermo Soto, I would have killed myself, mortal sin or not."

"Let's just be glad it's not going to come to that."

They sat there in silence for a few moments, sharing their sorrow over McLeod's passing. Finally, Rosa asked, "Was he in much pain . . . before he died?"

"I don't think so," Fargo lied. He didn't see any harm in it, and the next thing he said was the truth. "Mostly he was just worried about you."

A sad smile touched Rosa's face. "Yes. That is so much like him. He always worried more about others than about himself. What will be done with . . . with his body?"

"The colonel was going to take him on into the settlement. I reckon he'll be buried in Las Vegas."

"As good a place as any. He had no real home, for many years now. He was a wanderer." She looked at Fargo. "Much like you, I think, Skye."

"Yeah, we were both pretty fiddle-footed," Fargo agreed. "Always wanted to see what was on the other side of the next hill—"

He stopped short as sounds came to him through the early morning air, drifting down from the rim of the gorge above them. Voices called back and forth to each other in Spanish. Fargo recognized them, and so did Rosa. She let out a little gasp of surprise.

"Guillermo and his father!" she said. "They have found us!"

9

Fargo came to his feet and motioned for Rosa to be quiet. The Ovaro knew better than to nicker to other horses if he caught their scent, although the horses belonging to the Sotos would probably react if they smelled the stallion.

Fargo reached down and picked up the Henry, which he had placed beside the blankets earlier in the night. He didn't think they were in any immediate danger. If the Sotos and their men intended to explore the gorge of the Colorado, they would have to find one of the trails first, then carefully make their way down it. That would take time.

He was disappointed, though, that they were even over here in this area, instead of searching in the direction of Las Vegas. Either old Victorio was smarter than Fargo had given him credit for, which was a possibility, or they had gotten lucky and spotted some tracks by moonlight and followed them here.

Fargo was fairly certain of one thing: Guillermo wasn't the one who had found them. He didn't think the arrogant young bravo had that much skill or cunning. Guillermo was too accustomed to having everything handed to him.

Rosa stood up and came to Fargo's side. "Skye, what are we going to do?" she asked in a whisper.

"Sit tight for now," he told her. "They might not know we're down here. They could decide they're on the wrong track and ride away."

"Do you really think that will happen?"

He gave her a taut smile, although she might not have been able to see it in the predawn gloom. "I wouldn't bet against my luck."

But even the Trailsman's luck ran in short supply sometimes. A few minutes later, they heard a clatter as rocks tumbled down into the gorge and landed about a hundred yards away.

"They found the trail," Rosa breathed. "They've started down."

Fargo knew she was right. He could track the Sotos' movements by the sounds they made, and they were definitely descending into the gorge.

"We'd better move," he said.

He handed the rifle to Rosa while he saddled the Ovaro, listening to keep track of the progress their enemies were making as he did so. He estimated that the Sotos were less than halfway to the bottom of the gorge by the time he and Rosa were ready to go.

Fargo took the rifle back from her and grabbed the stallion's reins with his other hand. Without talking now, he gestured for her to follow him as he started along the ledge that bordered the river.

The sand on the ground was a result of the times in the past that the Colorado had flooded. Fargo wished it were thicker, so that it would do a better job of muffling the Ovaro's hoofbeats. He hoped they would blend in with the sound of the river. The hoofbeats of the Soto horses were louder because their steel shoes were striking the stone trail.

Fargo stayed in the lead. He didn't know how far the ledge ran, or if it stayed as wide as it was here. If it disappeared completely, or even narrowed down too much, they were trapped. All they could do was keep moving forward, though. It was too late to go back.

Behind them, a triumphant shout rang out. Fargo recognized the old man's voice, even though he couldn't make out the words. He could guess what had brought on Soto's excitement, however. The pursuers had reached the bottom of the trail and found the droppings left behind by the Ovaro. They knew that someone was down here in the gorge, someone riding a shod horse, so it had to be a white man rather than an Indian.

Fargo looked over his shoulder and saw a faint glow. They had lit a match or some sort of torch and were studying the ground. They would find the two sets of footprints, including one belonging to a woman, and would know that they were closing in on their quarry.

In a quiet voice, Rosa asked, "They're going to come after us, aren't they?"

"Yeah, they are." That wasn't the end of the bad news, either, Fargo thought.

The ledge was getting narrower. It was only about twenty feet wide now. That was still plenty of room for two people and a horse, but it was a bad trend.

The sky above the gorge lightened even more, and as it did, Fargo could see just how bad things were. Up ahead, the ledge continued shrinking. Over the next fifty yards or so, it narrowed down to no more than five feet.

Fargo glanced across the river. The ledge on the other side was still nice and wide, but that didn't do them a damned bit of good. He and the stallion might be able to swim that current, but he doubted that Rosa could. It would be a long shot even for him and the Ovaro.

He paused and said, "All right, Rosa, you go ahead of me now. Take my horse's reins and lead him."

"What are you going to do, Skye?"

"Don't worry," he said with a smile. "I'll be right behind you. But if anybody needs to fight a rearguard action, it'll have to be mè."

"I can use a gun."

"No offense, but not like I can. Anyway, you'll have a job to do, too. You have to be sure-footed, because this ledge gets mighty narrow up ahead."

She swallowed. "All right. I can do it." She reached for the reins and took them from him.

More excited shouts echoed from the walls of the gorge. Like hounds baying on the scent of a fox, Fargo thought. And like those hounds with a fox, the Sotos would tear him apart if they got the chance.

The sky above the gorge had turned orange. The sun was either already up or would be within minutes. When Fargo looked back the next time, he saw a flicker of movement. Although the walls of the gorge were rugged, the river ran mostly straight through here, and as a result, Fargo could see several hundred yards back downstream.

The men who were pursuing them could see him, too. He got confirmation of that when a rifle cracked and a slug smacked into the rocks above his head to go screaming off up the canyon.

"Don't shoot!" Guillermo shouted. "Hold your fire! You might hit Rosa!"

That was the same thing he had said the night before, but there was a difference this morning. Old Victorio yelled, "Kill them! Kill them both!"

Fargo heard the startled exclamation that cold-blooded order jolted from Guillermo. Then he couldn't hear anything except the deafening echoes of his own shots as he blasted three rounds from the Henry back downstream, working the rifle's lever smoothly between each shot.

"Keep moving!" he called to Rosa as the echoes continued to bounce back and forth between the walls of the gorge. He didn't know if he had hit any of their pursuers. He hoped he had. They had opened the ball and called the tune, and now they could dance to it as well. From here on out it was kill or be killed, Fargo knew.

Because that old man was loco.

Fargo backed away, snapping shots every time he saw somebody move. Between shots, he glanced over his shoulder and saw Rosa hurrying along the ledge, leading the stallion. More bullets came from the vaqueros. Some of the slugs smacked into the side of the gorge and sent dust and rock splinters flying in the air. Others ricocheted off, and those high-pitched whines added to the cacophony of sound inside this giant slash in the earth.

"Skye!" Rosa suddenly cried, and Fargo heard the alarm in her voice. He spun around, thinking that she must have been hit, but he saw instead that she had come to an abrupt halt.

And for good reason, because just ahead of her, the ledge narrowed even more, until it was no more than a yard wide.

"Skye, we can't . . . It's not wide enough . . ."

There was a lull in the firing from the pursuers. Fargo heard Soto and Guillermo shouting at each other in Spanish. The constant echoes made the words hard to understand, but Fargo made out enough to know that they were arguing about Rosa. Guillermo wanted to spare her life and insisted that he still loved her. Soto claimed that she was evil because she was the spawn of Jim McLeod.

"What about her mother?" Guillermo cried as the echoes faded enough for Fargo to hear the words. "You once loved her!"

"Once—but she betrayed me!" Soto shot back. "There is no more love, no more mercy in me. The girl must pay for the sins of her father and mother both! What they did to me must be avenged!"

"Is it not enough to kill McLeod?"

"Better still," Soto said, "to kill him after I have told him how his beloved daughter died at my hands!"

Rosa could hear the argument as well as Fargo could. She whispered, "Señor Soto is mad!"

"Like an old lobo wolf," Fargo agreed. "His hate's finally eaten him up inside. He can't think straight anymore."

But Fargo could, and what Soto had just said told him that the old man hadn't ordered Jim McLeod's death after all. Soto believed the mountain man was still alive. That meant the ambush on the ore wagons didn't have anything to do with Rosa's kidnapping, except that maybe Soto had found out somehow that Colonel Drummond was going to be starting to Las Vegas with the wagons and had assumed that McLeod would be with him. That meant Soto and his men would face lighter odds at the Lily Belle Mine when they went after Rosa.

Fargo didn't have time to ponder all the implications of what he had just heard. He and Rosa were still in great danger. Soto and Guillermo wouldn't stand there arguing all day. Soon the vaqueros would come out from behind the boulders where they had taken cover and resume stalking their prey.

"You heard them," Fargo said to Rosa. "Those vaqueros take their orders from the old man, not from Guillermo. If we surrender, they'll kill us both."

"You're saying we can't go back."

"We can make a stand right here and maybe go down fighting . . . or we can keep going and see where it leads us."

Rosa took a deep breath. "I say we keep going."

Fargo nodded. "Take it slow. I'll hold them off as best I can. At least I can make them duck a mite."

He waited until Rosa had moved out onto the narrower part of the ledge and coaxed the Ovaro to follow her.

Even the icy-nerved stallion was leery of venturing onto such a narrow path with the river racing past only inches away, but when Fargo said, "Go on, big fella," the Ovaro followed Rosa.

He brought the Henry to his shoulder and sent a couple more shots racketing down the gorge toward their pursuers. Judging by the amount of shots directed at him and Rosa, Fargo thought all six members of the group were still firing.

The two of them had been lucky so far, he told himself grimly, but that luck couldn't hold. It was only a matter of time before one of the bullets flying around found him, and then the Ovaro and Rosa would be hit, too.

Fargo's jaw tightened in the growing light. He had known for a long time that the perilous life he led made it likely he would die a violent death. That possibility didn't bother him all that much, because he wasn't the sort of man who wanted to die of old age, wasted and frail.

But there were still places he hadn't been, things he hadn't done, and besides that, he just hated to lose to a couple of no-good bastards like Victorio and Guillermo Soto. And down in a hole like this, too, where he couldn't see the sun or feel the wind on his face . . .

That thought made Fargo tilt his head back and look up toward the sky at the top of the gorge, and as he did, something caught his eye.

A rocky knob jutted out from the wall of the gorge, about thirty feet up. Fargo saw deep cracks rivening the stone wall above it. He studied the situation for a moment, then called to Rosa, "Keep moving! I'm staying here a spell!"

"Skye! No!" she protested. "I won't leave you! I won't let you give up your life to save me."

"That's not what I'm doing," Fargo said as he nestled

the smooth wood of the Henry's stock against his cheek. He sent another slug whistling down the gorge. "I think I know a way to stop them from following us!"

"Are you lying to me?"

"No! Now go! But leave the stallion here!" Fargo would need the Ovaro's strength if his plan was going to work.

Rosa let go of the reins and moved carefully but quickly along the ledge. Fargo sidled up to the Ovaro's rump and leaned forward to pluck the coiled rope from the saddle. He slid the rifle back in its sheath.

Bullets pinged off the rocks around him. The shots were coming closer now. He knew he didn't have much time. He shook out a loop in the rope, twirled it a couple of times, and then cast it at the projecting rock above his head.

The throw was short. The loop fell back down to the ledge. Fargo caught it and bit back a curse.

Tossing a lariat almost straight up like that was a mighty hard thing to do. Fargo wasn't in the habit of giving up, though. He stepped out to the edge, which gave him a slightly better angle on the throw.

It also gave Soto's vaqueros a better target for their shots. Fargo felt the wind-rip of a bullet's passage beside his ear as he swung the rope again and let fly with it.

This time the loop rose into the air and then came down over the knob, just as Fargo intended. He felt a surge of hope. He hauled down hard on the rope to make sure the loop was secure, then whipped the other end of the lariat around the saddlehorn.

"All right, fella," he told the Ovaro. "Straight ahead, and keep going."

Fargo gave the stallion a light slap on the rump to get him started. With careful steps, the Ovaro moved forward. The rope tightened.

"That's it," Fargo said. "Just keep right on."

The Ovaro seemed to have figured out what Fargo expected of him. He threw his considerable strength into the task. The rope grew even more taut, until it seemed to hum. Fargo knew he was imagining that. He wouldn't have been able to hear any such thing over the roar of gunshots, even if it existed.

But he heard the sudden cracking and scraping, followed by the rumbling crash as the protruding rock broke off and plummeted to the ledge. Some pieces splashed in the river. The rumbling continued as more pieces of heavily eroded rock that the knob had supported began to break off and fall as well.

Startled yells came from the vaqueros. Fargo didn't think any of them were close enough to be struck by the falling rocks, but the danger would certainly make them think twice about rushing Fargo.

He was starting to think twice himself about the wisdom of what he had done, because more and more rocks continued to break free and crash down to the ledge and the river. Fargo realized he had started a small-scale avalanche. That had been his intention, because he wanted to block the ledge and keep Soto from pursuing him and Rosa, but it was spreading faster than he had thought it would.

"We'd better get out of here," he said to the Ovaro. The rope was still attached to the rock that had pulled loose, which had fallen in the river and was acting as a drag on the stallion. Fargo jerked out his Arkansas toothpick. He hated to lose part of a good lariat, but he didn't have much choice. He slashed through the rope, grabbed the now free end, and called to the Ovaro, "Go!"

The stallion couldn't break into a gallop on such a narrow path, but he started moving faster. Fargo hurried after the horse as the rocks continued to fall behind him, almost at his heels.

A chunk of stone about the size of a man's head suddenly smashed into Fargo's left shoulder. He grunted in pain and struggled to maintain his balance as the impact sent him leaning toward the water. He might have been able to stay upright if at that moment his foot hadn't come down on a smaller piece of rubble that rolled under him. Fargo toppled off the ledge and fell into the Colorado River with a huge splash.

The water was cold as it closed over his head. He felt the current pulling at him like a million tiny hands, seeking to hold him down and bash the life out of him against the rocks that dotted the river.

Fargo still had hold of the lariat with one hand, though, and his grip tightened on it. He got his other hand around the rope and held on as if his life depended on it—because it probably did. If nothing else, the current could sweep him downstream so that he was once again in range of the guns wielded by the Sotos and their men.

Fargo's head popped up out of the water. He gulped down a lungful of air and then started pulling himself hand over hand along the rope. He looked back, saw that they were past the sweep of the avalanche, and called to the Ovaro to stop. A moment later, soaked to the skin and trembling from the cold, Fargo climbed out onto the ledge, in front of the Ovaro this time.

He leaned against the stallion's shoulder and caught his breath. Looking back along the ledge, Fargo saw the rubble heaped up on it high enough so that no one could get past it, at least not without going to a lot of trouble and running a lot of risk. He grinned as he heard angry shouts coming from beyond the rocks. Crazy old Victorio had to be realizing about now that his quest for vengeance had come to an abrupt end.

At least for a while. Fargo knew that he and Rosa still had to get out of this gorge somehow and make it back to

Las Vegas. Soto knew where they were. He might take Guillermo and the vaqueros back the way they had come and try to intercept Fargo and Rosa when they climbed out of the gorge.

First things first. He had to catch up to Rosa, and then they had to find a way out.

Fargo figured she couldn't have gone more than a few hundred yards while he was trying to pull down those rocks. With the light growing stronger, he thought he ought to be able to see her. He didn't, though, when he looked along the gorge ahead of him.

Could she have lost her balance and fallen in the river, only to be swept past him without him even noticing? Fargo didn't think that was very likely, but if she had hit her head on something when she fell, she might have been knocked out so that she couldn't call for help. Fargo's gut twisted at the thought of such a thing happening.

A moment later, though, he spotted her sitting on the ledge with her back to the rock wall and her knees drawn up. Her head hung forward in an attitude of despair.

Leading the Ovaro, Fargo hurried forward and called, "Rosa! Rosa, are you all right?"

She lifted her head and gave him a stricken look. "Skye," she said, her voice dull, "Skye, it's over."

"What are you talking about?" Fargo asked, but even as he spoke, he looked past her and saw the answer to his question.

The ledge disappeared just past her, ending in a jagged drop-off. They couldn't go forward, and with the rockfall blocking the path behind them, they couldn't go back.

They were trapped.

10

That thought didn't last long in Fargo's mind. He shoved it aside and started looking for a way out of this predicament.

He directed his first glance upward. His eyes searched for a path that he and Rosa could use to climb out of the gorge. The wall was too sheer, though. If he had been alone, he might have attempted the climb, but not with Rosa. Anyway, that would have meant leaving the Ovaro behind, and Fargo was damned if he was going to abandon his oldest friend in the world.

The river was all that was left.

"Listen to me," he said to Rosa. "We're going to get out of this."

"But how?" she asked. "There's nowhere to go."

"Stand up."

"What?"

"Stand up," Fargo repeated. When Rosa did, still looking confused and defeated, he stepped closer to her and had her raise her arms so that he could loop the rope around her body. He tied it securely.

By then, Rosa had figured out what he had in mind. "Skye, I . . . I can't swim."

"You won't have to. Just hang on to one of the stirrups and let the horse pull you through the water. The rope's just in case your hands slip."

"What are you going to do?"

"I'll be holding the other stirrup," Fargo said. "So I'll be close by, in case you get in any trouble."

"Is your horse strong enough to swim with both of us weighing him down?"

Fargo smiled and rubbed the Ovaro's shoulder. "He's got more sand than any horse I've ever seen, so I know he'll do his best. There's still a ledge on the other side of the river. If he can get us that far, that's all he has to do."

"But even if we make it, we'll be on the wrong side of the river. The gorge will be between us and Las Vegas."

"Right now, there is no wrong side of the river," Fargo pointed out. "We're just trying to stay alive."

"That's true." Rosa moved closer to him and put a hand on his arm. "Skye, I'm sorry I gave up for a minute. My parents raised me better than that. We'll keep fighting as long as we're alive."

Fargo grinned at her. "Darned right, we will. Are you ready?"

She summoned up a smile of her own. "As ready as I'll ever be, I guess."

Fargo took off his boots, tied them together, and then tied them to the saddlehorn. "We'll jump in first, but you come right after us," he said. "Don't hesitate. The current's liable to push us downstream before the stallion can start swimming hard enough to make any headway against it."

"All right. I understand." Rosa took a deep breath. "Let's go."

Fargo took a close grip on the Ovaro's reins and said, "I know you won't like this, big fella, but it's the only way." He pointed the horse's head toward the river, then yelled and slapped the Ovaro's rump. The stallion leaped from the ledge, and so did Fargo. They went into the river with a huge splash.

Once again, the chilliness of the water was a shock to Fargo. He fought it off, grabbed the stirrup on the Ovaro's left side, and looked up at Rosa.

"Come on!" he urged her. "Right next to me!"

Just like he had told her, she didn't hesitate. She jumped into the river feetfirst. That took a lot of guts, he knew, since she couldn't swim. She cried out as she hit the water. Then she went under.

Fargo kept one hand on the stirrup and used the other to reach for Rosa. He took a deep breath and plunged under the surface as he searched for her. His free hand brushed against her dress. He grabbed hold of it and kicked hard, propelling them upward. As they broke out into the air again, he slid his arm around her and pulled her close to him.

All three of them turned in the current as the Ovaro began fighting against the steady push of the water. Fargo helped a sputtering Rosa work her way around to the stallion's other side so that she could grasp the right-hand stirrup.

"Hold on!" he told her. "You can do it!"

She wrapped both arms around the stirrup, turned her frightened gaze over the Ovaro's back toward Fargo, and gave him a curt nod.

"Come on, fella," Fargo called to the stallion. "Get us to that other ledge!"

The Ovaro began swimming strongly toward the other side of the river, towing Fargo and Rosa with him. The current pushed all three of them back downstream, but the stallion struggled stubbornly against it and kept them from being swept away. Despite his best efforts, though, progress toward the far side was maddeningly slow. Fargo could tell that the horse was beginning to labor.

"You can do it," he told the Ovaro, just as he had Rosa. "Come on!"

Something plunked into the water, off to Fargo's left. He twisted his head around and saw that the current had pushed them far enough downstream so that Victorio and Guillermo Soto, along with the four vaqueros, could see them again. Flame spurted from rifle barrels as all the men except Guillermo opened fire on them.

Under the circumstances, Fargo couldn't fight back. All he could do was hang on to the stallion and hope that they made it to the other side before the flying bullets drilled any of them.

The ledge was closer now. Fargo risked letting go of the stirrup and swam for it on his own, his legs kicking and his arms cutting the water in powerful, lunging strokes. He reached the ledge first, grabbed it, pulled himself onto it. His pulse hammered in his head and his heart slugged wildly in his chest. He was out of breath, but there was no time to regain it now. He rolled over and grabbed the Ovaro's reins as the stallion made it to the ledge. It wasn't going to be easy for the stallion to climb onto the rocky path. Fargo leaned out and reached for Rosa with his other arm.

"Grab my hand!" he told her. She did, clasping his wrist as he clasped hers. A slug whined off the rocky wall above them. Fargo leaned back and hauled hard. Rosa came out of the water and sprawled onto the ledge.

The Ovaro had his front hooves on the ledge by now. Fargo grabbed the reins with both hands and leaned backward, putting all his strength into the effort to help the stallion. The big black-and-white horse managed to get one of his rear hooves on the ledge and lunged up, shedding water in torrents as he came out of the river.

Fargo waved Rosa upstream. "Move!" he told her. "We have to get out of range of their guns!"

Bullets continued to whine around them as they hurried

along the ledge. It was about eight feet wide here, not wide enough to be comfortable but much better than the trail they had been following on the other side of the river.

Within seconds, the shots died away. Angry shouts and curses in Spanish replaced them. Fargo knew what that meant—he and Rosa had made it far enough upstream that Soto and his men could no longer get a clear shot at them. They were safe again, for the moment.

Fargo kept moving anyway, leading the Ovaro and taking Rosa's hand. He wanted to get them well out of range before stopping.

They were all soaked, and down here in the gorge, out of the sunlight, the air felt chilly on their wet skin. That was another reason to keep moving. They would stay warmer that way.

"Skye, can't we stop now?" Rosa asked. "They can't shoot at us anymore, can they?"

"Not without climbing up on those rocks and risking dislodging them," Fargo replied. "That would send them right into the river, and I don't reckon even Soto wants to take that chance, loco as he is. But we'll keep going for a while anyway, just in case."

"All right," she agreed, but the dubious tone of her voice made it clear that she didn't really understand.

The ledge varied in width from eight to twelve feet, so they didn't have any trouble following it. When Fargo estimated that they had walked about a mile, he said, "We can stop for a while now."

"Good," Rosa said. "I'm exhausted. And cold."

A few hardy bushes grew out of the rock along here. That was another reason Fargo had chosen this place to stop. While Rosa sat down with her back against the gorge wall to catch her breath, Fargo unsaddled the Ovaro, then gathered some branches that had broken off those bushes. Floods in the past had left pieces of driftwood wedged among the rocks, and Fargo picked up those as well.

"I'll build a fire so we can maybe dry off a little," he said.

"How will you do that?" Rosa wanted to know. "Didn't the river ruin your matches?"

"Not all of them," Fargo told her with a smile. "Anyway, you don't have to have matches to start a fire. The Indians managed for a long time before somebody came up with the idea of a match. Most of 'em still do."

"Somehow, I'm not surprised that you can start a fire without matches. I'm sure my father could have, too."

Fargo nodded. "Sure he could have, probably better than me. Jim McLeod knew how to survive in the wilderness, that's for sure."

"It's too bad he had more trouble with civilization," Rosa said with some bitterness in her voice.

Fargo couldn't disagree with that. He opened his saddlebags instead and dug out a small leather cylinder that he had sealed with pitch. A wooden plug also coated with pitch was stuck in the open end of the cylinder. He pried it out and removed a small bundle wrapped in oilcloth. When he unrolled the oilcloth, he revealed half a dozen matches.

Hunkering on his heels, Fargo arranged the branches and driftwood he had found and used one of the matches to get a fire going. It wasn't very big, but the warmth that came from the flames was welcome anyway. Rosa came over and huddled next to it with him.

After a few minutes, she said, "We'd be better off out of these wet clothes, Skye."

Fargo knew she was right. He nodded and stood up to peel off the buckskin shirt. "I'll turn my back if you want," he offered.

"That's not necessary." Rosa stood, too, and turned

around so that her back was to Fargo. "If you'll just undo these buttons . . ."

Fargo unfastened the buttons as she asked. Rosa slid the dress off her shoulders and pushed it down over her hips. As it fell around her feet, she reached down to grasp the hem of her shift and pulled it over her head. Since she had turned away from Fargo, he had a good view of her golden brown legs, amply rounded buttocks, and smooth back. It was a mighty nice view, he had to admit, even though he still felt a little uncomfortable enjoying it.

Rosa turned around to face him again. Her high, full breasts had the same burnished golden tone as the rest of her body, except for the large, brown nipples. The thick triangle of raven black hair between her legs drew Fargo's eyes to it. She stood there before him, nude and unashamed, and said, "I thought you were going to take your clothes off, too, Skye."

A low growl came from Fargo's throat. Rosa was old enough and experienced enough to know what she was doing. He had tried to be considerate of her feelings, but clearly, there was something more going on here than just an attempt to warm up after being drenched in the river.

Fargo's hands went to the buckle of his gun belt.

Within moments, he had removed the gun belt, taken off his boots, and stepped out of his trousers so that he was just as nude as Rosa. She moved toward him. He said, "If you're doing this because you feel grateful to me—"

"I *do* feel grateful to you, Skye, but that's not the reason. I'm doing it because I've wanted you ever since the first time I saw you, and because, despite everything, we're *alive*."

Fargo knew exactly what she meant and understood the feeling. Nothing made a fella appreciate and savor all the good things life had to offer more than a brush with death. Both of them had heard the deadly song of bullets passing close by them today, and before that, they had known the sharp stab of grief over Jim McLeod's death. That grief would not be lessened or cheapened if they were to take comfort in each other, Fargo sensed.

He put his hands on her shoulders and drew her closer to him. She tilted her head back and lifted her face to receive his kiss as he brought his mouth down on hers. Their bodies molded together, her breasts flattening against his chest. As their lips parted and their tongues met, Fargo slid his hands down from her shoulders to her hips and pressed her even more tightly to him. The thick shaft of his erect manhood prodded her belly.

The kiss lasted for a long moment, growing more intense and urgent as it went on. Rosa's hands explored Fargo's back and roamed down to his buttocks. Finally, Fargo broke the kiss and said with a wry smile, "Those bedroll blankets are all wet, and this ledge is going to be mighty hard and uncomfortable."

"We'll make the best of it," Rosa said with a smile of her own.

Fargo took the saddle off the Ovaro and placed it on the ground to use as a pillow for his head, even though the leather was wet. He stretched out on his back. Rosa sat down next to him and leaned over to brush her lips against the head of his shaft as it jutted up from his groin. She cradled the thick pole of flesh in both hands and ran her tongue around the tip. Fargo groaned at the sensations that heated caress provoked within him.

Rosa opened her lips, took the head in her mouth, and sucked gently on it. Fargo closed his eyes as waves of pleasure washed through him, their current even stronger than that of the Colorado River. When he opened his eyes again, he reached up and cupped one of her heavy breasts in his hand. His thumb stroked the hard brown nipple.

Rosa moved her lips from his member and started kissing his belly. She worked her way up his body, pausing to tongue each of his nipples. She wound up lying on top of him, with her legs straddling his hips. He slipped his shirt and trousers under her knees to protect them as much as possible from the hard ledge.

She kissed him again as he spread his hands on the rich curves of her rear end, kneading and caressing them. Her hips pumped so that the hot wetness of her sex rubbed along his shaft. Fargo throbbed and knew that Rosa must feel it against the sensitive folds.

She sat up and poised herself above him, then reached down to grasp his manhood and position the tip against her opening. Her hips lowered so that he slid slowly into her, filling her inch by inch. Feeling the delicious heat of her body enclose him made Fargo forget for the moment about everything that had happened, all the sorrow and hardship they had both endured in the past couple of days. For right now, and for as long as they were joined like this, the world went away and nothing was left of it except the two of them and this desolate gorge and the intimacy they were experiencing.

When Fargo was fully sheathed inside her, Rosa sat there, her eyes heavy-lidded and a slight smile on her lips. A long sigh of pleasure came from her.

"That feels so good, Skye," she whispered. "Feeling you in me like this makes everything else go away. Like nothing bad can touch us here."

"Don't tempt fate," Fargo warned her with a chuckle. From this angle, he could cup both of her breasts and run his thumbs over the nipples, so he did just that and greatly enjoyed it. So did she, judging by the look on her face.

Her hips began to move, slowly at first and then faster and faster. Fargo's hips lifted so that he met her thrusts with thrusts of his own. Even though this was the first time they had made love, instinct helped them match their movements. Within moments they had fallen into the timeless rhythm of passion.

Fargo's hands moved from Rosa's breasts and cupped her perfect face instead, drawing her down so that he could kiss her as he continued driving his manhood in and out of her. Her hands clutched his shoulders in growing excitement. Her hips pumped harder and harder.

She moved her hands to his chest and levered herself up into a sitting position again. Now she rode him at a gallop, caught up in a frenzy of arousal. Fargo felt much the same way himself. His hands clasped her thighs to steady her as he pistoned up into her again and again. At last Rosa closed her eyes, threw her head back, and let out a low, throaty cry as her culmination rippled through her, causing her belly to spasm.

Fargo let himself go as well, delving as deeply into her as he could and then freezing there as his climax erupted from him in a series of throbbing jets. Rosa cried out again as his juices filled her.

Then she sagged forward, resting on his broad chest. Fargo put his arms around her and folded her into a firm embrace. A long, satisfied sigh came from Rosa.

"I wish it could have gone on forever," she whispered.

"So do I," Fargo said. "So do I."

He kept holding her, and somewhere along the way, both of them fell asleep in each other's arms, at the bottom of the Colorado River gorge.

The sun beating down in Fargo's eyes woke him. Squinting against the glare, he looked up and saw the fiery orb edging into the strip of sky visible above the gorge. That meant it was midday, and he and Rosa had been asleep for several hours.

He stirred, and she murmured sleepily as she shifted in his arms. Then she lifted her head, blinked her eyes open, and said, "Skye?"

"We're all right," he told her. "Might ought to get up and move around a little, though. Work the kinks out."

A throaty laugh came from her. "I'd say we worked out some of the kinks already." As if to demonstrate the truth of her statement, she slid a hand over his belly and groin, then clasped her fingers around his hardening shaft.

Fargo laughed, too, as he caressed her breasts. In a matter of moments, Rosa had shifted around so that her head was poised over his manhood and her thighs were parted just above Fargo's face. They began to pleasure each other with lips and tongues, and it wasn't long before their culmination surged through them. Rosa's thighs clasped hard around Fargo's head as he drove his tongue into her. At the same time, his hips lifted from the ground as he emptied himself into her mouth. Eagerly, she swallowed his hot juices.

When both of them had caught their breath, they stood up. Fargo spread their still-damp clothes on some rocks to dry in the sun, which wouldn't be shining directly into the gorge for very long. Then he got out his Colt and the Henry and started breaking down, cleaning, and drying them.

"I don't suppose you have any more jerky, do you?" Rosa asked as Fargo hunkered on his heels next to the flat rock where he was working on the guns.

"Worked up an appetite, did you?" he asked as he glanced up at her with a grin. She gave him an impish smile of her own.

Neither of them had forgotten about Jim McLeod's

death, and the pain of his loss would last a long time before fading, but they were also practical enough to know that they had to keep moving forward and not spend too much time looking back.

"I have a little left," Fargo told her. "In that saddlebag over there."

Rosa found the single strip of jerky and tore it in half with her teeth, then gave one piece to Fargo. He told her that she could have all of it, but she insisted on sharing.

"We're in this together, Skye. Either both of us will make it back safely . . . or neither of us will."

Fargo appreciated that sentiment. He felt the same way.

He got the revolver and rifle back together while he was gnawing the small piece of jerky. When he and Rosa had washed down their meager meal with river water, Fargo checked their clothing and found it mostly dry. Although he hated to see her cover up that magnificent body, he said, "I reckon we'd better get dressed. We still have to find a way out of this big hole in the ground."

"As uncomfortable as it is, I almost wish we could stay here forever," Rosa mused. "That way, we wouldn't have to go back to the rest of the world."

Fargo knew what she meant. As long as they were alone down here, they could pretend that her father's death, Guillermo's obsession with her, and Soto's hatred for both her and McLeod didn't exist. When it was just the two of them, those troubles didn't matter.

But, of course, they would starve to death. Anyway, Fargo knew the feeling of splendid isolation wouldn't last. Already, he was trying to figure out some way to see that the Sotos faced justice for what they had done. There was also the matter of finding the outlaws who were responsible for McLeod's death.

He just had too much to do to spend the rest of his life

making love to Rosa, Fargo told himself—no matter how pleasant that prospect might seem at the moment.

When they were dressed, Fargo saddled the Ovaro. They bid farewell to their camp and walked northward along the ledge. The sun gradually disappeared past the western rim of the gorge. Even though it was no longer shining directly down on them, Fargo knew that they still had hours of daylight left in which to find a way out.

That might not be long enough. Fargo knew that it could be miles between trails leading to the top of the gorge. The ledge might peter out before they reached one. A natural rockfall might have blocked their path. There could be all sorts of obstacles to their escape.

But they still had hope, and for the Trailsman, that was enough to keep him going. They pushed on through the afternoon, Fargo leading the Ovaro and walking side by side with Rosa where there was room on the ledge. In the places where it narrowed down, they moved along the path in single file. On each of those occasions, Fargo was concerned that the ledge might end, as the one on the western bank of the river had, but that didn't happen.

By the time Fargo estimated that they had traveled for at least five miles, Rosa was exhausted and her feet hurt from walking on the rocky ground. Fargo, a born horseman, didn't care much for hoofing it that far, either. But when Rosa said dejectedly, "We're never going to get out of here," Fargo shook his head.

"Just a little farther," he told her. "You never know what we'll find just around the next bend of the river."

That was true. A few hundred yards farther on, the Colorado took a turn to the east, and just past that bend, the river widened out into a pool of sorts, where the current wasn't as fast. Not only that, but a few cottonwood trees grew around the pool, forming an oasis.

The reason the pool was there was because a sandbar

and a line of rocks extended across the river, forming a natural dam. Fargo's heart leaped with excitement when he saw that, because the barrier not only slowed the river's current and formed the pool, but he and Rosa could also use it as a makeshift bridge to cross the Colorado. That solved one of their problems.

The steep, winding trail that went back and forth up the stone wall on the western side of the gorge solved the other.

Fargo gripped Rosa's arm and pointed. "There it is," he told her. "Our way out."

"Oh, Skye!" She threw her arms around his neck and hugged him. "You knew we would find it, and we did."

Fargo grinned. "A little luck goes a mighty long way toward making a fella's confidence look good. If he turns out to be wrong, he's just a stubborn, damn fool."

Crossing the river was tricky. Fargo went first, jumping from rock to rock, then feeling out the sandbar and finding the best places to walk as the current swirled the water around his calves. He pointed out the route to Rosa as he crossed, being careful and telling her exactly where to step when she came across.

Once he was on the other side, Rosa took a deep breath and started after him. Fargo wished he had been able to tie his lariat to the Ovaro's saddle horn and stretch it across the river so that Rosa would have something to hang on to, but the rope was too short for that now.

She held her arms out from her sides to balance herself as she stepped across the rocks until she reached the sandbar. Fargo knelt on the far bank and watched her progress closely, repeating the instructions he had given her earlier as he was crossing. After what seemed like longer than it probably was in reality, Rosa was within reach. Fargo stood up and leaned toward her. She clasped his outstretched hand and he pulled her up onto the bank.

Rosa hugged him briefly. He could feel a slight trembling in her body. She had been scared because she was unable to swim, and he couldn't blame her for that. If she had slipped, she would have plunged into the river, and he might not have been able to get to her in time.

But that didn't matter now. She was across the river safely, and they were together again.

Fargo whistled for the Ovaro. The stallion started across the river without hesitation, picking his way with instinctive skill, much as Fargo had done. Once the horse reached the bank, Fargo rubbed his nose and congratulated him.

"Any reason not to head on up?" he asked Rosa.

She shook her head. "I'm anxious to get out of this place. I want to see some open sky again." A shudder ran through her. "Traveling through this gorge is like being in a grave that never ends."

Fargo hadn't thought about it that way, but he could see that she was right. He would be glad to see the open sky again, too.

It took them more than an hour to follow the zigzagging trail to the top. The Utes or their ancestors had probably hacked it out in centuries past. The steep climb forced them to stop a couple of times along the way so that Rosa could rest. A few minutes' breather didn't do Fargo and the stallion any harm, either.

At last they walked past a cluster of boulders and emerged onto the vast plain that bordered the gorge. The sun hadn't quite set yet, but it was low on the western horizon and painted the heavens in a beautiful panoply of blue, purple, red, orange, and gold. It was as pretty a sunset as Fargo had seen in quite a while, and coupled with finally escaping from the great gorge of the Colorado River, the sight did a lot to lift his spirits. Rosa must have felt the same way, because she threw her arms around him and hugged him in sheer exuberance.

That nice moment didn't last long. It was ruined a couple of seconds later by the sudden blast of a shot and the high-pitched whine of a bullet ricocheting off one of the boulders a few feet away.

11

Fargo heard another shot and the flat *whap!* of a slug passing close to his ear. He grabbed Rosa and twisted away, putting both of them behind one of the rocks. As he dragged her down into cover, he shouted, *"Hyyaaah!"* at the Ovaro. That sent the stallion galloping along the lip of the gorge, out of the line of fire. A couple of bullets kicked up dust behind the Ovaro as the horse raced out of range.

Unfortunately, the Ovaro took Fargo's rifle with him. That left Fargo armed only with the Colt and the Arkansas toothpick. He and Rosa were pinned down, with too much open ground in front of them and the gorge behind them.

They could have retreated back down the trail, Fargo knew, but if they did that, Soto and his vaqueros might be able to stand at the top of the path and fire down at them. Not only that, but after just getting out of the gorge, Fargo was in no mood to descend into it once more.

He had no doubt that Victorio Soto was responsible for this ambush. Soto must have taken his men and ridden north to the first trail that led out of the gorge, in the hope that Fargo and Rosa would reach it and climb out of the great gash in the ground. It had been a good guess. That was exactly what had happened.

"Skye, what are we going to do?" Rosa asked in a fearful voice. Fargo detected an undercurrent of anger in her tone, too.

"Do you want to go back down in the gorge to try to get away from them?" he asked.

"After we just got out of there?" She shook her head, and now Fargo saw more anger than fear in her eyes. "Besides, I'm tired of running from Guillermo and his father. They've made my life miserable for years now." Her defiance faded, and her shoulders drooped. "But what else can we do?"

"We can make them come to us," Fargo said. "They can't get behind us or even flank us. All they can do is come straight at us. And if they do that, they're going to pay a high price."

Their enemies had one other option, which was to wait them out. Fargo and Rosa had no food or water.

He didn't mention that possibility because he didn't think it would happen. Victorio Soto didn't have the patience for a long siege. Besides, night would soon be falling, and there was always a chance that Fargo and Rosa could slip around them and get away in the darkness.

No, Soto wouldn't wait, Fargo decided. The old man was too bitter and full of hate to do that.

As they lay behind the boulder, Fargo drew his Colt and thumbed a cartridge from his shell belt into the gun's empty chamber. As a precaution, most men who packed iron carried only five rounds in their guns, leaving the sixth chamber empty so that the hammer could rest on it. That was the surest way for an hombre to make certain he didn't shoot his own foot off.

But when a fight was looming, a smart man filled that unused chamber. The extra shot might make all the difference in the world.

"Give me your knife," Rosa said between clenched teeth. "If they make it this far, I want to be able to fight, too."

For a second, Fargo had thought she intended to use the

131

Arkansas toothpick to kill herself rather than allow Soto and Guillermo to capture her if he was killed. Such a thing wasn't unheard of, out here on the frontier.

But he should have known better, he thought with a wry chuckle as he slipped the big knife from its sheath and handed it to her.

"You are amused?" she asked.

"Only at myself, for thinking something when I should have known better."

She didn't ask him what he was talking about. Maybe she knew. It didn't matter.

"Fargo!" The cracked old voice belonged to Victorio Soto and came from a small rise about a hundred yards away. "Fargo, can you hear me?"

"I hear you!" Fargo shouted back. He didn't think Soto would have anything to say that he wanted to hear, but he was willing to listen.

His hunch proved to be correct. Soto called, "Give me the girl, and your death will be fast!"

"You reckon that's enough to get me to turn her over to you? You'll just kill her, too!"

"No!" Soto insisted. "I will give her to my son! Guillermo has left me, but he will come back for the girl!"

Fargo glanced over at Rosa. She shook her head emphatically.

"No, Skye," she said. "I'd rather stay here and die fighting than be a peace offering from that crazy old man to his son."

Fargo nodded. "That's what I figured you'd say. I'm surprised Guillermo took off like that. He must've been really upset when his father told his men to shoot you, too."

"Fargo!" Soto yelled again.

"No deal!" Fargo told him. "Rosa stays with me!"

"She dies with you, then!" Soto screamed. A second

later, Fargo heard the old man yelling orders in Spanish, commanding his vaqueros to mount up and charge the rocks where Fargo and Rosa had holed up.

The men must have been reluctant to do that. Fargo heard an added stridency in Soto's voice as he repeated the orders. Then Soto cried, "Follow me, or die in your beds like women!"

The insult did the trick. When Soto boiled over the top of the rise a moment later, charging on horseback toward the rocks, the four vaqueros were right behind him. In fact, they surged ahead of him, closing ranks in front of him to protect him. He was their patron, and their code of honor would allow them to do no less. Powder smoke spurted from the muzzles of their rifles as they closed in on the rocks.

Fargo and Rosa kept their heads down. Fargo heard the bullets slamming into the boulder and whining off, sometimes bouncing among the other rocks. He held his fire, knowing that the Colt had a much shorter range and that he probably wouldn't have time to reload. He had to make every shot count.

That was why the vaqueros seemed to be almost on top of them by the time Fargo finally rose up and opened fire. Coolly, he ignored the bullets whipping around his head and drew a bead on the rider who was in the lead. The revolver roared and bucked in Fargo's hand. The vaquero slew backward in the saddle, dropping his rifle and grabbing at the horn in an attempt to stay mounted.

He failed. His fingers slid off the saddle horn, and he toppled off the running horse, screaming as he fell right under the slashing hooves of one of the other horses. That rider hauled on his reins and tried to avoid trampling his companion, but it was too late.

Even worse for the second rider, his horse's legs got tangled. The animal went down hard, crashing to the ground. The luckless vaquero, who tried to kick his feet free of the stirrups and get off the horse before it was too late, wound up with two thousand pounds of horseflesh rolling over him.

Fargo caught a glimpse of that mishap from the corner of his eye as he shifted his aim and fired again. Another vaquero flew off his horse, this time with blood spraying from his head where the Trailsman's bullet had slammed into it. Three men were down, and he had only used two bullets. Luck was with him.

Then, as it so often did, that luck proved fickle. Something burned across Fargo's upper-left arm, knocking him halfway around just as he squeezed off a shot at the fourth and final vaquero. His bullet went wild. The bullet's impact had knocked his aim off.

"Skye!" Rosa cried in alarm as she saw the blood on his arm. She started to stand up.

"Stay down!" Fargo told her. He dropped to a knee as another slug whined past him. Fighting off the pain from his wounded arm, he lifted the Colt and triggered again. He had to angle the shot upward, since the last vaquero was right on top of them.

The bullet struck the man in the throat and bored up into his brain. Blood spurted from a severed artery as the vaquero flipped backward out of the saddle.

Fargo lunged up and caught the reins of the man's horse. They could use it for Rosa to ride. He struggled to control the animal. The gunfire and the sharp tang of powder smoke had spooked the horse.

Pounding hoofbeats reminded him that Victorio Soto was still alive. The old man had fallen behind the vaqueros as they charged, but now he screamed curses as he approached. His old cap-and-ball pistol boomed. The lead ball was so heavy and traveled so slowly compared to a bullet that it hummed as it went past Fargo's ear, rather than whining.

Fargo still had two shots left. He snapped one at Soto, but at the last second Soto swerved his mount. Fargo knew he had missed. He tried to draw a bead for his sixth and last shot, but before he could, Soto was there among the rocks with him and Rosa. Soto twisted in the saddle and fired at Rosa, who dived aside as the ball knocked rock dust from the boulder beside her.

She still held Fargo's Arkansas toothpick. She leaped up and slashed at the old man's leg with it. Fargo had to hold his fire because he couldn't risk hitting Rosa instead of Soto.

Rosa's strike missed Soto, but the knife cut deeply across the horse's flank. The animal let out a scream of pain and leaped backward, rearing up as it did so. Soto yelled and hauled back on the reins, but he was too weak to stop the maddened horse. Out of control, it went over the edge of the gorge, carrying Soto with it.

Fargo heard shrieks from both man and horse. As he stepped to the brink, Fargo looked down and saw Soto and the horse tumbling through the air toward the river, a couple of hundred feet below.

He turned away, having no interest in seeing what was going to happen when they landed.

Rosa stared at him, her eyes wide with horror. "Skye!" she said. "I didn't mean . . . I didn't know the horse would . . . *Dios mio!* Not even on a madman like Soto would I wish such a thing!"

Still holding the Colt, Fargo went to her and pulled her into his arms. He held her as she pressed her face to his chest and trembled for a long moment. As her breathing steadied, he said, "Soto would have killed us both. He's tried often enough, the past couple of days. You had every right to defend yourself, Rosa. Don't ever forget that."

He felt her nod. "I know," she said quietly. "I know that. But still, to die that way . . ."

"Let's concentrate on living, not dying," Fargo told her. To that end, he let go of her and reloaded his Colt, keeping an eye on the sprawled bodies of the four vaqueros as he did so.

As soon as he had a full wheel in the revolver again, he checked the bodies and found that all four of Soto's men were dead, just as he had thought. Their horses had run off about a quarter of a mile and then stopped to try to graze on the sparse grass dotting the landscape.

A whistle brought the Ovaro trotting back to Fargo. He mounted up and told Rosa, "Wait here. I'll see if I can round up one of those other mounts for you."

"But you're hurt," she protested with a nod toward his bloodstained arm.

"You can bandage it up when I get back. I want to catch at least one of those horses."

Actually, he caught all four of them before he was finished. It was a long ride back to Las Vegas, and Fargo figured it wouldn't hurt to have some extra mounts. They could make better time that way.

When he had brought the horses back, Rosa cleaned the bullet crease on his arm with water from one of the canteens, then tied a rag around it as a makeshift bandage. Then Fargo helped her onto one of the horses. She nodded toward the dead vaqueros and asked, "What about them? Do we just leave them here like this?"

"Not much else we can do," Fargo said. "I don't have a shovel or anything else to dig with, and anyway, I'm not much inclined to spend hours hacking out a hole in this hard ground for some hombres who did their level best to kill me."

"That's true," Rosa said. "I understand. But I also know that they were just following their patron's orders."

"That was their mistake," Fargo said.

"What about Guillermo?"

That question brought a frown to Fargo's face. "The old man said Guillermo left him. I reckon he must have ridden off by himself after they climbed out of the gorge south of here. There's no telling where he is now. On his way back to Santa Fe, I hope."

"His father is dead. My father is dead . . ." Rosa sighed. "If it pleases *El Señor Dios*, let this be the end of it."

"Amen," Fargo said.

They rode away from the gorge of the Colorado without looking back.

As late in the day as it was, Fargo and Rosa didn't get very far before they had to stop and make camp, but neither of them wanted to spend the night in that place of death beside the great gorge. They found tortillas and jerky in the saddlebags on the vaqueros' horses, so they were able to fill their empty bellies this time. Fargo didn't build a fire. Now that they were back out in the open, he didn't want to risk attracting the attention of any hostiles who might be in the area.

It was inevitable that they would wind up sharing their blankets. They made love again, this time with Fargo on top as Rosa lay back and spread her thighs wide to receive him. At first, he kept the pace slow and easy, but as their arousal grew, so, too, did the speed and power of his thrusts into her. By the time he finally spent inside her, both of them were bucking and breathing hard.

When they were done, they went to sleep in each other's arms, with the Ovaro standing by to alert Fargo if any enemies came too close.

The next day, Fargo set a course to the northwest, toward Las Vegas. Since they hadn't really talked about it, he asked Rosa, "What are you going to do now?"

"Now that my father is gone, you mean? I have no family, other than some of my mother's relatives in New Mexico. I suppose I could return there and they would take me in, but we have never been close." She smiled. "I could travel with you."

"I'm not sure that would be a good idea," Fargo said. "I tend to roam around a lot, and trouble seems to have a way of dogging my trail."

Rosa laughed. "And you are a man who generally rides alone, except for that horse of yours. I know that, Skye. My father was much the same way. You would never be happy with me tagging along after you."

"Doggone it, that's not exactly the way it is—" Fargo began.

"But close enough. I'm sorry, Skye. I knew when I said it that it could never be like that. Perhaps I just wanted to see what you would say."

Fargo was quiet for a moment; then he said, "I'd be glad to take you back to New Mexico. We can stock up on supplies in Las Vegas and head out in that direction."

"Perhaps. But I was thinking about asking Colonel Drummond if he would like for me to continue cooking for him and his men at the mine."

Fargo nodded. "That's not a bad idea. The colonel seems like a good hombre, and he'll keep his men in line. I'm sure your cooking is a heap better than anything they could muster up, too."

"How would you know?" she asked with a laugh. "I have never cooked for you."

"Well, maybe we can do something about that, once we get back to Las Vegas."

"I'd like that," Rosa said.

They didn't reach the settlement that day, but Fargo

knew they would the next day. Once again, he and Rosa made camp and shared their blankets, thoroughly exploring each other's body before they fell asleep.

When they set out the next morning, Fargo expected to ride into Las Vegas by midday. He was right about that. The sun hadn't quite reached its zenith by the time he spotted the splash of green in the surrounding tan and brown landscape that marked the location of the springs. A short time later, he was able to see smoke rising from the chimneys in town.

"We made it, Skye," Rosa said as she saw the settlement ahead of them, too. "In a way, I'm almost sorry."

He glanced over at her. "Why would you be sorry?" he asked.

"Because now that we're here, you'll be leaving me and riding on."

"Not for a while yet," Fargo assured her. "I don't intend to leave until after you've talked to Colonel Drummond and made sure that you've got a place at the Lily Belle. If he's not in town, it may be several days before he shows up with another ore shipment."

Fargo wondered if the ore wagons had made another trip from the mine while he was gone, and if so, whether the outlaws had attacked them again. He was looking forward to talking to Drummond.

"And you'll want to pay your respects to my father and see that he received a proper burial."

Fargo nodded. "I sure will. I think we can trust the colonel to have taken care of that, but I'd like to see for myself."

He intended to run to ground the men responsible for Jim McLeod's death and see that they got what was coming to them. Rosa didn't need to know that right now, though. If she did, she might insist on coming along with him, and that would just make his job harder. There would be time enough to tell her about it when justice had been done.

As they entered the settlement, one of the first people Fargo saw was Colonel Henry Drummond. The tall, ramrod-straight former military man had just come out of the livery stable when he spotted Fargo and Rosa and strode toward them.

"Thank God!" Drummond exclaimed. "I heard that Rosa had been kidnapped and that you had gone after her, Fargo, but I didn't know if you'd succeed in rescuing her." He paused beside the horse Rosa was riding and reached up to clasp her hand. "Are you all right, Miss McLeod?"

"I'm fine, Colonel," she assured him, then nodded toward the Trailsman and added, "Thanks to Skye."

"I'm sure." When Fargo had dismounted and helped Rosa to the ground, Drummond shook Fargo's hand and asked, "Was it the Sotos who raided the mine and took her?"

"That's right," Fargo said.

"Where are they now? Are they liable to come after her again?"

"Not unless they can come back from hell. The old man and the four vaqueros are dead. I don't know where Guillermo is, but he seems to be gone."

Drummond frowned. "Not to sound too bloodthirsty, but I might feel better about the situation if you had told me that the young man was dead, too."

Fargo felt the same way, even though he didn't think that Guillermo would be loco enough to come after them on his own, without his father to goad him on and those vaqueros to back his play.

You never could tell what a fella in love—or a fella who *thought* he was in love—might do, though.

Drummond turned to Rosa again and said, "Miss

McLeod, I'm very sorry about what happened to your father. I was so relieved to see that you're all right, the loss that you've suffered slipped my mind for a moment. You have my sincere sympathy."

"Thank you, Colonel."

"And although under the circumstances I certainly wouldn't blame you for refusing, your job at the mine is waiting for you if you'd care to return."

Rosa smiled. "Skye and I were talking about that yesterday. That's exactly what I want to do, Colonel."

"Splendid!"

Fargo said, "I reckon you must've gotten your next ore shipment to town all right, Colonel."

Drummond grimaced. "Not exactly."

"You were attacked by those outlaws again?" Fargo asked sharply. If that was the case, he might be able to pick up their trail right away.

"There hasn't been another shipment," Drummond said with a shake of his head. "One of the wagons broke an axle on the way into the settlement on that last trip, after Mr. McLeod's unfortunate death, and I've been waiting for a replacement to be crafted." He nodded toward the barn behind him. "The liveryman also does work like that, but he's not very fast about it, to say the least. He assures me the wagon will be ready to go tomorrow, though. I thought it best to wait and return to the mine with all three, although I've ridden out there and back myself while the two of you were gone."

"Skye!"

The excited voice made Fargo look around. Lily Drummond hurried toward them, a smile on her face. That smile faltered slightly when Fargo moved enough for Lily to see Rosa standing beside him. But then she came on and embraced him.

"I was so worried when Henry told me you'd gone after those men who raided the mine," she said. "I see you found Miss McLeod and brought her back."

"That's what I set out to do," Fargo said.

Lily laughed. "And Skye Fargo always does what he sets out to do."

"Well . . . maybe not always. But I give it my best shot."

"I'm sure you do." Lily turned to her brother. "Henry, we have to have Mr. Fargo join us for dinner tonight . . . and Miss McLeod, too, of course."

"That's an excellent idea," Drummond agreed. "We'll have the hotel put on the best spread that the dining room is capable of."

Fargo wasn't sure it was such an excellent idea, even though he liked the prospect of a good meal and spending some time in Lily Drummond's company.

But things had changed between him and Rosa since the last time he'd seen Lily, and the slight hesitation in her voice when she invited Rosa to dinner told Fargo that she might realize that. The idea of sitting down at a dining room table with two women, each of whom he had made love to in the past week . . .

Well, it was a mite interesting, anyway, Fargo thought.

12

Colonel Drummond insisted on renting rooms at the hotel for both Fargo and Rosa. Since Rosa didn't have any of her belongings with her except the clothes on her back, Drummond wanted to buy her a nice dress for that evening, too, and asked Lily to lend a hand with that.

"I'm sure the selection at the local mercantile is quite limited," the colonel said, "but perhaps you can help Miss McLeod pick something out."

"Of course, Henry," Lily said, but again Fargo noticed a subtle reluctance that Drummond obviously didn't. Still, Lily was gracious about it. She took Rosa's arm and went on. "Come with me, dear. I'm sure you've had a perfectly awful time the past few days, and you need some normal female activity to do, like shopping for a new dress."

Fargo figured that normal female activity would depend on the female, but he didn't say anything as he watched Rosa and Lily walk down the street toward the general store. Maybe if they spent some time together they would start to like each other.

He hoped that they wouldn't get too friendly and start comparing notes about certain things, however.

"Come down to the Silver Queen with me," Drummond said to Fargo once the women were gone. "I want to hear about what happened."

Fargo was amenable to that suggestion. Once he'd seen

to it that the Ovaro and the other horses were taken care of at the livery stable, he and Drummond availed themselves of the free lunch at the saloon. They nursed beers while Fargo told the colonel about rescuing Rosa from her captors, all the way up to the showdown with Victorio Soto and the four vaqueros at the edge of the great gorge.

"What a harrowing experience for Miss McLeod," Drummond said when Fargo was finished. "I'm a bit surprised she's willing to stay out here. I wouldn't blame her if she wanted to return to her home in Santa Fe."

"That's just it," Fargo said. "Her home's not in Santa Fe anymore. With both her folks gone, she'll have to make a life of her own."

"Until some young man snatches her up and makes her his wife."

"I've got a hunch it'll take a pretty good hombre to do that," Fargo said.

Drummond chuckled. "You wouldn't have any trouble accomplishing that goal if you wanted to, my friend."

Fargo shook his head. "I'm mighty fond of Rosa, Colonel, but I travel in single hitch, not double."

"Your loss, if I may be so bold as to say so."

"You know, Colonel, some of the time I agree with you," Fargo said.

A short time later, he went back to the hotel and claimed the key to the room Drummond had rented for him. The past several days had been mighty hard ones, and Fargo was grateful for the chance to stretch out on the bed and sleep for a few hours. His body needed the rest.

When he woke up around dusk, he felt refreshed. He washed up and dressed in his spare buckskins. He still had to buy a new hat, because it felt a mite strange going around without a Stetson on his head.

When he had picked up his key earlier, he had inquired as to which room Rosa was in. He went to the door of that room now and knocked on it. From the other side of the panel, she asked who was there, and he said, "Fargo."

Rosa opened the door right away, a big smile on her face. She looked lovely in a dark blue gown. Back east, the style was probably outmoded already, but here on the frontier, the dress looked very fashionable.

"Skye, isn't it beautiful?" she said as she turned around for him.

"Beautiful is the word, all right," Fargo agreed with a grin. "And the dress is nice, too."

Rosa laughed. "You don't have to flatter me. You know that anything I have is already yours. It *is* a nice dress, though. I'm grateful to Colonel Drummond."

"He's a mighty decent hombre," Fargo said. He had detected some definite warmth in Drummond's voice when the colonel was talking about Rosa. The notion that the two of them might wind up together wasn't all that far-fetched. True, Drummond was considerably older than Rosa, but such matches were common on the frontier. More important, Fargo thought that Drummond would probably treat her decently, and she certainly deserved that.

"I'm glad I decided to go back out to the mine. Rugged as it is, I'd rather be there than in Santa Fe."

Fargo offered her his arm, and together they went downstairs to the lobby. They found Drummond waiting there. He greeted them and said, "Lily should be here any minute now. She said she had a few more items to take care of down at the office, and then she'd join us."

"She's really diligent about the business, isn't she?" Fargo asked.

"No doubt about that," Drummond said emphatically. "She handles it all—getting the ore assayed, dealing with the government on the silver contract, keeping track of the profits . . . there's no way I could get along without her."

"I reckon the mine's doing well?"

"Very well, according to Lily's figures. Well enough that I'm really torn about that offer from the mining syndicate. After that last attack on the ore wagons and Mr. McLeod's tragic death, I was ready to sell out. Now that I've thought it over, though, I'm not so sure anymore."

"What does your sister want to do?" Rosa asked.

Drummond chuckled. "As hardheaded and practical as Lily is, I think she'd prefer that we sell out while there's a good offer on the table. She's been pointing out to me that there's no way of knowing when the vein of silver that I found will peter out. And that's true enough. There's something to be said for striking while the iron is hot, as the old saying goes."

"You're the only one who can decide that, Colonel," Rosa said, "but I sort of hope that you don't sell, at least right away. I'm looking forward to going back out to the mine."

"Well, then, that helps me make my decision, doesn't it?" Drummond said with a smile. He held out an arm to Rosa. "Why don't we go on into the dining room? We can wait for Lily there. I really can't imagine what's keeping her."

Once they had sat down at one of the tables, Fargo said to Rosa, "The colonel and I were down at the Silver Queen earlier, and it reminded me . . . did either of the Sotos say anything about trying to bushwhack me that night when Kelly was killed?"

Rosa frowned as she thought about the question. After a moment, she said, "Not that I remember. I don't think either of them ever mentioned anything about that."

Drummond said, "I thought it was generally accepted that that miner, Duffy, was responsible for the attack on your life and for Mr. Kelly's death."

"Yeah, but with Duffy dead in that cave-in, we never

found out for sure if he was the one who took those shots at me," Fargo pointed out. "Even if we eliminate the Sotos as suspects, we still can't be positive that Duffy was to blame."

"Of course, none of it can be changed now, regardless of who was behind the ambush," Drummond pointed out. "Life has moved on."

"It's got a habit of doing that," Fargo agreed. He was still curious, though.

The three of them chatted for another quarter hour. Then Drummond said in an irritated voice, "I can't understand why Lily isn't here by now. I think I'll go down to the office and see what's keeping her."

Something occurred suddenly to Fargo. Guillermo Soto was still on the loose, and the young man could have followed him and Rosa here to Las Vegas. Guillermo might want to settle the score for his father's death. Lily Drummond was a possible hostage Guillermo could use against him, Fargo realized.

Without revealing what he was thinking, Fargo came to his feet before Drummond could and said, "Why don't you let me go check on her, Colonel? I wouldn't mind stretching my legs a mite, and you can stay here and visit with Rosa."

Both of them looked pleased with that idea. Drummond said, "Very kind of you, Fargo."

He wasn't doing it out of kindness, Fargo thought as he left the hotel. He believed it was a real long shot that Guillermo would go after Lily, but just in case that had happened, Fargo figured he could handle trouble like that better than the colonel.

Night had fallen over the settlement while Fargo, Rosa, and Drummond were talking in the hotel. Out of habit, Fargo kept a close eye on the alleys as he walked along the street, but nobody took any potshots at him.

At first, he thought the building housing the office of the Drummond Mining Company was completely dark, which worried him. If Lily wasn't there and wasn't at the hotel, then where was she?

But then he noticed the yellow glow in a small window at the rear of the building. Fargo didn't know what was back there—a storage room, maybe—but he circled toward it anyway, intending to knock on the rear door.

The window was open several inches, enough so that Fargo heard voices inside the building as he passed it. Those voices froze him in his tracks.

The first one belonged to a man, and Fargo didn't think he had ever heard it before. "—not enough," the man was saying. "I'm taking the biggest risk here, so I deserve a bigger share."

"So you intend to blackmail me for it?" The second voice, despite being colder and harder than Fargo had heard it before, belonged to someone he knew.

Lily Drummond.

"That would be a mistake, Coleman," she went on.

Coleman, Fargo thought. He had seen the name somewhere . . . After a second, he remembered. It was on the sign of the local assay office. Alonzo Coleman was the name of the assayer.

"Look, if people ever find out what I've been doing—" Coleman went on.

"Then don't let them find out," Lily cut in. "This is going to be over soon. My brother will—"

This time it was the assayer who interrupted. "Your brother will never sell out," Coleman said. "He's too damned stubborn. He thinks he's found a real silver strike that's going to make both of you rich."

"You're wrong. After those ore wagons are attacked again, he'll give up. He can't stand to have his men killed."

Every muscle in Fargo's body tensed. A part of his mind wanted to reel in shock from what he was hearing, but as the pieces of the puzzle snapped together in his brain, he knew it was true. Lily was behind the attacks on the ore shipments. She was trying to force her brother to sell out to the mining syndicate.

There was another reason for the attacks, Fargo realized. Outlaws wouldn't try to steal the ore unless those shipments were valuable—or unless someone wanted folks to *believe* they were valuable. The syndicate wouldn't doubt that the Lily Belle was a profitable mine. Desperadoes wouldn't keep going after the ore wagons unless that was the case, now would they?

It all made sense. Lily controlled the company's books. She could alter them to make it appear that the mine was producing more silver than it really was. Drummond wouldn't know the difference. He freely admitted that Lily handled everything on that end of the business. He wouldn't know how much they were really making from the government, either. Again, that was Lily's bailiwick, not his. She had taken him in completely, and not only him. The representatives of the mining syndicate had been fooled, too.

That meant those gunmen who had jumped the wagons were working for her. She was the one truly responsible for the death of Jim McLeod.

That truth made Fargo sick right down to his core.

It was going to practically destroy the colonel.

But Drummond had to be told what was going on. He deserved to know what his sister had done, and he had a right to know that the mine wasn't nearly as profitable as he thought it was, too. Just how close it was to worthless, Fargo had no idea, but Coleman, the man who assayed the ore, would know, and Fargo had a feeling that Coleman would crack under pressure and tell everything he knew.

Fargo put his hand on the butt of his Colt and took a step toward the rear door. He intended to bust in there, get the drop on Coleman and Lily, and force them to come with him back to the hotel, where Coleman could explain the whole plan to Drummond.

Before Fargo could reach the door, though, a shape loomed up out of the darkness and thrust a gun at him. Fargo heard the weapon's hammer go back. Then Guillermo Soto said, "Do not move, Señor Fargo. I would very much like to shoot you right now."

Fargo almost drew the Colt anyway, but instinct stopped him. As fast as he was, he couldn't pull the gun and fire before Guillermo put a bullet through his head.

"I hear Señorita Drummond in there," Guillermo went on. "Knock on the door."

"What do you want with her?" Fargo asked.

"I know that Rosa is at the hotel with the colonel. He will turn her over to me if I have his sister."

That was exactly what Fargo had been worried about earlier—before he discovered just how treacherous Lily Drummond really was.

Now he stalled for time, saying, "You followed us here from the gorge of the Colorado, didn't you, Guillermo? You've been spying on Rosa and me, waiting for your chance to get back at us."

"She spurned my love," Guillermo said, his voice thick with emotion, "and then she killed my father. And you helped her, Fargo. For those things, you both will die."

"That won't bring your father back. And Rosa can't love you if she's dead."

"I have already given up on that," the young man choked out. "Now I want only vengeance."

The rear door of the office suddenly opened. Lily stepped out and said, "I'll help you, Señor Soto. You don't have to kidnap me."

Startled, Guillermo jerked back, turning toward Lily as he did so. That took his gun off Fargo, who would have drawn his own Colt except for the fact that Lily now had a gun leveled at him.

"Don't do it, Skye," she snapped. "I don't want to kill you, but I will if I have to."

"You tried hard enough," he said in a flat voice, "the night you bushwhacked me and killed poor Kelly instead."

Her eyes widened in the lamplight that spilled out around her. "My God. How much do you know?"

"All of it," Fargo said. "How you've been fooling your brother, how you tried to make the mine seem more valuable than it really is, even how you killed Duffy and caused that cave-in so nobody would know he'd been murdered. He made a convenient scapegoat for Kelly's shooting, didn't he?"

That last was a guess, but the way Lily's mouth tightened and hatred burned even brighter in her eyes confirmed it for him. "I didn't want you poking into my affairs, Skye," she grated. "I know your reputation. But then, once Henry went back to the mine with that old man and his bitch of a daughter, things changed. It didn't seem quite so urgent that I get rid of you. I thought perhaps you'd just move on without finding out what I'd been doing."

"I came close to doing just that," Fargo told her. "But you overplayed your hand. Once Jim McLeod was killed, I wasn't going to rest until I found out who was responsible. I would've gotten to it sooner, if not for this boy and his obsession with Rosa."

"Boy!" Guillermo said. "I am a man! I loved her!"

"And now you hate her," Lily said coolly. "Well, so do I. I want her gone, and Fargo, too. So do you. It's to our advantage to work together, Señor Soto."

Guillermo nodded his head. "*Sí.* I understand."

So did Fargo. Coleman hadn't said anything or put in an appearance, but Fargo knew he hadn't left the office. The assayer was hiding in there. Lily must have heard him and Guillermo talking out in the alley and ordered Coleman to lie low.

He had to give her credit. She was fast on her feet, putting together a plan in a matter of seconds that would result in him and Rosa both dying, thus clearing the way for her to continue with her plan to prod her brother into selling the mine. At the same time, she would get rid of Rosa, a potential rival for Drummond's affections.

And here he'd thought that Lily was jealous of Rosa because of *him*, Fargo told himself.

To accomplish her goals, Lily planned to use Guillermo as her weapon. She'd said she didn't want to kill Fargo, but she wouldn't mind a bit if the young man did it for her. Then Guillermo would die, too, because Fargo was convinced Lily had ordered Coleman to follow them to the hotel, wait until violence erupted, and then gun down Guillermo once he had killed Fargo and Rosa.

That would leave Lily with a clean slate, except for the minor problem of Coleman wanting a bigger payoff for himself once Drummond sold the mine. Fargo was sure Lily could handle that.

She'd just find some other damned fool to kill Coleman for her.

This had to end, Fargo thought, and the only way to accomplish that was to get everything out in the open.

That was why he didn't try to fight when Guillermo ordered him to turn around. Fargo complied with the order. Guillermo stepped up close behind him, jabbed the gun in his back, and plucked Fargo's Colt from its holster.

"Do as the señorita says," Guillermo told him. "Go to the hotel."

Lily lowered her pistol and slid her hand into the pocket of her dress. "I'm going to pretend to be your prisoner, too, señor. Just be sure that when we get to the hotel, Fargo and Rosa both die."

"Why don't you just have him murder your brother, too?" Fargo asked as they walked up the alley toward the street. "For that matter, why haven't you already murdered him yourself? Then you could do whatever you wanted with the mine."

Lily laughed softly. "You may not believe this, Skye, but I actually do love my brother. I don't want to see anything bad happen to him. I just want him to stop throwing away what little money we have left on that damned mine. This is the only way we can recoup what we've lost on it."

"How come you didn't just tell him from the start that the mine wasn't producing enough silver to make it worthwhile?"

"I tried to," she said. "He wouldn't listen to me. He swore that it was going to be a jackpot. Henry is a stubborn, stubborn man."

Having been around Colonel Drummond, Fargo didn't doubt that. The colonel believed in his dream of being a silver baron.

The three of them reached the street and turned toward the hotel. Lily walked at Fargo's side now, her hand in her pocket, and he knew she had the pistol cocked and aimed at him.

"When we get there, call Rosa out," Lily said quietly to Guillermo. "Henry will come with her, so be careful. I don't want any harm to come to him."

"I will do my best, señorita," Guillermo said, "but I cannot promise anything."

Fargo glanced back. Guillermo had lowered his gun and now held it unobtrusively alongside his leg so that the other people on the street wouldn't be as likely to notice it. Fargo considered whirling around and jumping the young man, but he knew if he did, Lily would shoot him and later claim she had been trying to hit Guillermo instead. The showdown had to be postponed another few minutes.

They reached the hotel. Guillermo raised both his gun and his voice, calling out, "Rosa! Rosa McLeod! Come out! I have Fargo!"

A tense moment passed. The few people who were nearby saw Guillermo's gun, now pressed against Fargo's back, and gave the young would-be killer plenty of room.

Fargo took advantage of the opportunity to say to Guillermo, "She's going to double-cross you, too, you know. She's got a man following you, ready to gun you down as soon as you've done her dirty work for her."

"That's insane," Lily said coldly. "Don't listen to him, Señor Soto."

"It's the truth," Fargo insisted. "If you help her, you're a dead man."

Guillermo snapped, "Shut up, gringo." Then he shouted again, "Rosa!"

The door of the hotel opened. Rosa stepped out, jerking loose from Colonel Drummond's grip as she did so. The colonel had tried to stop her from exposing herself to danger, which came as no surprise to Fargo. Drummond stepped onto the porch right behind her, gun in hand.

"Guillermo, what are you doing here?" Rosa said. "Has there not been enough death and tragedy already? Go home. Please."

"I have no home," Guillermo said, his teeth bared in a grimace. "I have no father, no woman to love me . . . and you are to blame!"

The gun barrel went away from Fargo's back. He

twisted and saw Guillermo jerk the weapon toward Rosa. He shouted, "Coleman, now!"

It was a calculated risk. The assayer was no professional gunman. He was also nervous as hell, Fargo knew from the conversation he had overheard earlier. Sure enough, Coleman was lurking in the darkness about twenty feet away, just as Fargo suspected, and hearing the order, the man reacted without thinking, firing from the shadows behind Fargo, Lily, and Guillermo.

Fargo lashed out and knocked Guillermo's arm up as he fired. At the same instant, Coleman's bullet thudded into the young man's back. The impact knocked Guillermo forward a step so that his face was only inches from Fargo's as his eyes widened in pain and shock and the realization that Lily had indeed double-crossed him.

Guillermo had tucked Fargo's Colt behind his belt. As Guillermo fell, the Trailsman grabbed the revolver and pulled it free. In the light from the hotel, he saw Lily turn her gun toward him and fire. Flame stabbed from the pistol's muzzle. Fargo felt the bullet tug at his shirt as he threw himself aside.

Panic-stricken, Coleman ran forward and fired again, this time at Fargo. But his aim was off, and Lily cried out instead as she staggered. From one knee, Fargo triggered his Colt. The slug caught Coleman in the leg, spinning him off his feet. He screamed in agony and dropped the gun as he clutched at his bullet-shattered thigh.

Drummond bounded off the porch, crying in horror, "Lily!" She had crumpled to the ground with both hands pressed to her stomach. Fargo saw the blood crawling over her fingers like fat, black worms.

Fargo stood up and kicked away the gun Lily had dropped. Then he reached Coleman's side in a couple of long strides and picked up the assayer's gun.

Coleman looked up at him and pleaded, "Help me. I'm hurt. I'm going to bleed to death!"

"Not if I can help it," Fargo said. He reached down with his free hand, grasped Coleman's arm, and hauled the man to his feet. Coleman cried out again as Fargo half marched, half dragged him toward Drummond, who was bent over his sister, distraught. "You'll live to confess everything that's been going on here."

Rosa came down from the porch and rested a hand on Drummond's shoulder. As Fargo came up with his prisoner, she turned toward him instead.

Fargo looked down, saw Lily's wide, staring, lifeless eyes, and shook his head at Rosa.

"Stay with the colonel," Fargo said. "He's going to have some hard things to face up to, and he'll need a strong woman beside him."

Rosa hesitated, then nodded and put her hand on Drummond's shoulder again. The fingers tightened as she said, "I'm here, Henry. I'm here."

Fargo sat the sobbing Coleman down on the edge of the porch and looked at the scene in the street, the sprawled bodies of Lily and Guillermo, the grief-stricken Colonel Drummond, the curious onlookers gathering. . . .

Las Vegas wasn't much of a town yet, and maybe it never would be, but it was enough to make Fargo long for the mountains, far from so-called civilization and the taint of greed and sin it always brought with it, everywhere it went. He would be there soon, Fargo told himself, answering the big, clean call of the frontier.

LOOKING FORWARD!
The following is the opening
section of the next novel in the exciting
Trailsman **series from Signet:**

THE TRAILSMAN #338
TEXAS TRACKDOWN

Texas, 1860—
where danger for the Trailsman
lurks in the untamed land beyond the Brazos.

The sound of a ruckus somewhere nearby made the big
man in buckskins narrow his lake blue eyes. He paused on
the steps of the brick courthouse in Weatherford, Texas,
and looked for the source of the commotion.

The shouting came from a saloon on the south side of
the courthouse square. Men hurried in that direction to see
what was going on. Just as one hombre reached the saloon's entrance, the batwings flew open and made him
jerk back. A man came backward out of the saloon, stum-
bling on the rough planks of the boardwalk as he tried to
keep his balance.

He failed in that effort and landed in the street. A small
cloud of dust rose around him from the impact. He shook

his head, evidently trying to clear some of the cobwebs from his brain.

On the courthouse steps, Skye Fargo leaned against the railing and folded his arms across his broad, muscular chest. A faint smile touched his wide mouth as he shook his head. Some folks just shouldn't patronize saloons. They always got into trouble when they drank. Evidently, the fella who'd landed in the street was one of them.

A man slapped the batwings aside and stalked out of the saloon. Two more men followed closely behind him. The first man was big, with massive shoulders and long arms. A black beard jutted from his chin and hung down over his chest. He stepped into the street, reached down and grabbed the fallen man's shirt.

Fargo's eyes narrowed even more as the big man hit his victim twice, back-and-forth blows with a malletlike fist across the hombre's face. Then the man drew back his foot and kicked that unfortunate son in the belly. He kicked him again, making his body bow up and then roll through the dust. The big man's companions stood on the boardwalk in front of the saloon, laughing and yelling encouragement.

"Go get him, Sabin!"

"Stomp his guts out!"

Shaking his head again, Fargo went down the steps to the hitch rail in front of the courthouse. He reached for the reins of a magnificent black-and-white Ovaro stallion tied there.

"Stop it! Get away from him!"

The sound of a woman's voice shouting in anger and fear made Fargo pause and turn his head to look toward the saloon again. The woman was rushing toward the violence in the street from a general store also on that side of the square. Her sunbonnet had slipped down, revealing blond hair. She was young, no more than twenty or so.

She tried to get between the big man called Sabin and the man he had knocked down. Her fists flailed at him. Sabin snarled and clamped a hamlike hand on her shoulder. He flung her out of his way like a rag doll. With a cry of pain, the young woman sprawled in the street, too.

When Fargo saw that, his jaw clenched under the close-cropped dark beard. Instead of untying the Ovaro's reins, he patted the horse on the shoulder as he strode past and said, "I'll be back."

The distraction provided by the young woman had given the man in the street time to struggle to his feet. He was young, too, maybe twenty-five, with curly brown hair. As Sabin turned toward him again, he lunged forward and swung a fist at the bigger man's head.

Sabin slapped aside the blow before it reached its target and then hooked a punch into the young man's belly. He laughed, grabbed the young man's shoulders, and head-butted him in the face. Blood welled from the man's nose. He collapsed when Sabin let go of him.

"Now comes the real stompin'." Sabin lifted a foot and poised it, ready to drive his bootheel down into the young man's face.

Fargo's voice came from behind him. "I don't think so. Leave him alone."

One of Sabin's friends on the boardwalk called out a warning. "Watch out, Sabin!"

The big man looked around anyway, just in time for Fargo's fist to explode on his jaw. Fargo was several inches shorter and thirty or forty pounds lighter than Sabin, but he packed a lot of strength into his powerful frame. The punch landed cleanly and sent Sabin flying off his feet. He crashed down in the dirt street, just like the man he had been beating.

Fargo flexed his fingers to make sure he hadn't busted anything in his hand. Everything seemed to still be working properly.

Sabin's friends stared as if they were unable to believe that anybody had knocked the big man down. Their eyes bugged out even more when Sabin tried to get up and failed. He slumped back down with a groan.

Even so, Fargo didn't turn his back on the man. He kept his eyes on Sabin as he angled toward the young man and woman. Another woman had appeared, probably coming from the general store as well, and with an anxious look on her face now knelt beside the blonde. This one was younger, eighteen or so, and had light brown hair in braids.

"Jessie, are you all right?" the brunette asked. She looked over at the young man. "Oh, Whit, what have you done now?"

With help, the blonde sat up. She brushed some of the dust off the front of her dress, which pulled the calico fabric tighter and emphasized the curve of her breasts.

"I'm fine. Stop fussing over me, Emily. Whit's the one who's hurt."

She got to her feet, and the two young women went over to the young man called Whit. Fargo had gotten a good enough look at all three of them to recognize the family resemblance. The young women had to be sisters, and Whit was their brother.

Quite a few people had gathered to watch the fracas. Now that it was over, they started to drift away. That didn't surprise Fargo. None of them had stepped forward to help Whit. All they had been interested in was watching.

Fargo gave a polite tug on the broad brim of his brown Stetson as he stepped up to the two young women. "Ladies. Let me give you a hand with this fella."

"Thank you." The blonde managed to flash a quick smile at him, but she still looked upset and worried. "I hope he's not hurt too bad."

Fargo reached down, got his hands under Whit's arms, and lifted him to his feet. The lower half of the young man's face was smeared with blood, but at least his nose didn't appear to be broken. He was lucky in that respect.

Whit swayed and would have fallen, but Fargo still had hold of him and kept him upright.

"He probably needs to sit down somewhere."

The brunette pointed and said, "That's our wagon over there."

Fargo steered Whit toward the vehicle. Whit was pretty unsteady, but with Fargo's help, he made it to the wagon. The tailgate was already down, so Fargo sat him on it and kept a hand on his shoulder to steady him.

"Emily, you go see if you can get a wet cloth so we can clean him up." The blonde gave the order like she was used to being in charge. She looked at Fargo and went on. "I'll stay here with Mr. . . . ?"

"Fargo. Skye Fargo."

"I'm Jessie Franklin. That's my sister, Emily, and this is our brother Whit."

Fargo smiled. "I'd say that I'm pleased to meet you, Miss Franklin, but under the circumstances . . ."

"Well, *I'm* pleased," Jessie said. "If you hadn't come along, that monster might have killed poor Whit."

Fargo hadn't smelled any liquor on Whit's breath as he was helping the young man over to the wagon. He asked, "Do you have any idea what started the fight?"

"Unfortunately, I do." Jessie Franklin took a deep breath. "I'm afraid I did."

Sabin's companions stepped down from the boardwalk and hurried over to their fallen friend. One of them, a little fox-faced man, reached down and shook his shoulder.

"Sabin! Sabin, you better get up and whale the tar outta that bastard. Sabin!"

The big man just groaned again. The one who had just tried to rouse him looked over at the third man and said, "We got to do somethin' about this!"

The third man shook his head, with a dour expression on his saturnine face. "Did you see the way that fella walloped Sabin? I don't want any part of that. Let's just pick him up, get him back in the saloon, and pour a drink down his throat. That's what he needs."

The second man took his battered old hat off and scratched his head, which was covered with lank, fair hair. "Well, all right, but it don't set well with me, lettin' that varmint get away with hittin' our compadre like that."

"Come on, Martin. Quit your bellyachin' and give me a hand with him."

Together, they struggled to lift the semiconscious Sabin to his feet, and then the three of them staggered off toward the saloon. Once they were inside, Martin and the third man helped Sabin sit down at an empty table. Martin handed a coin to his companion.

"Go get us a bottle, Jackson."

"Sure."

Martin took one of the other chairs at the table while Jackson went off to the bar. Sabin pressed his palms against the table for support as he ponderously shook his head.

"What the hell happened out there?" he said.

Martin leaned forward eagerly. "Some big fella in buckskins cold-cocked you—that's what happened. Don't you remember?"

"I don't remember nothin' except goin' out in the street to teach that damn Franklin kid a lesson."

Martin licked his lips. "Well, this other hombre, he came up and hit you from behind. With a two-by-four."

Sabin took hold of his bearded jaw and gingerly worked it back and forth. "If he hit me from behind, how come it's my jaw that hurts?" His voice was thick with pain.

"That's because he, uh, he came up on you from behind, but then you turned around just as he swung that board at your head."

"Oh." Sabin frowned. "What happened to the kid?"

"He went off with the fella that walloped you. And those pretty little sisters of his."

Jackson came back from the bar with a bottle of whiskey and three glasses. "Martin, you ain't agitatin' again, are you?" he asked as he thumped the bottle and glasses down on the table. "I swear, you like to stir things up more'n anybody I ever saw."

"I was just tellin' Sabin here about how that other fella came up and hit him from behind with a two-by-four." Martin looked meaningfully at Jackson as he spoke.

"What? Oh. Yeah." There was a resigned tone to Jackson's voice now. "A two-by-four."

Sabin spoke with a rumble like thunder. "Well, hell. I can't let him get away with that."

"You sure can't." Martin grinned. "Want me to go see if I can find him for you so you can settle the score?"

Sabin reached for the bottle. "Maybe in a little while. I

got to get some of this Who-hit-John in me first. I got a devil of a headache." He splashed some of the fiery liquor in a glass, then threw back the drink. He ran his tongue around his whiskery mouth to collect any stray drops. "But he ain't gonna get away with it. That's for damned sure."

No other series packs this much heat!

THE TRAILSMAN

**Follow the trail of the gun-slinging heroes of
Penguin's Action Westerns at
penguin.com/actionwesterns**

From
Frank Leslie

THE GUNS OF SAPINERO

Colster Farrow was just a skinny cow-puncher when
the men came to Sapinero Valley and murdered his
best friend, whose past as a gunfighter had caught
up with him. Now, Cole must strap on his
Remington revolver, deliver some justice, and
make a reputation of his own.

THE KILLING BREED

Yakima Henry has been dealt more than his share of
trouble—even for a half-white, half-Indian in the
west. Now he's running a small Arizona horse ranch
with his longtime love, Faith, and thinks he may
have finally found his share of peace and prosperity.
But a man from both their pasts is coming—with
vengeance on his mind...

**Available wherever books are sold or at
penguin.com**